Croatian Nights

Croatian Nights

A festival of alternative literature

*Edited by Borivoj Radaković,
Matt Thorne and Tony White*

Translation by Celia Hawkesworth

First published in 2005 by Serpent's Tail,
4 Blackstock Mews, London N4 2BT
website: www.serpentstail.com

Designed and typeset by Sue Lamble
Printed by Mackays of Chatham, plc

10 9 8 7 6 5 4 3 2 1

Contents

Grateful thanks to the Ministry of Culture of the Republic of Croatia for its generous support.

Acknowledgements

The editors would like to thank the contributors, Pete Ayrton of Serpent's Tail, Celia Hawkesworth, Lesley Thorne, Nenad Rizvanović, Hrvoje Osvadić, Kruno Lokotar, Dražen Kokanović, Jurica Pavićić, Ante Tomić, Ivo Brešan, Magdalena Vodopija, Roman Simić, Đermano Senjanović, Stanko Andrić, Franci Blašković, Drago Orlić, Ivica Buljan, Zoran Kujundžić, Vesna Svilokos, Borka Pavičević, Vukan Lazarević, Lisa Gooding, Kate Tull, Ruth Petrie, Motovun Film Festival, all of about 80 authors that read with FAK, Irvine Welsh, James Kelman, Barry Gifford, Richard Berry, Joško Paro, Flora Turner, Suzanne Joinson, the clubs Voodoo, Gjuro 2, Palach, Uljanik. The editors would also like to thank Robin Evans and Roy Cross from the British Council in Zagreb, and the Croatian Ministry of Culture for supporting the costs of translation.

Introduction

Tibor Fischer

Are there big countries and small countries in the world of literature? *Croatian Nights* gives you the chance to make up your mind. On the one hand you have a country of sixty million, covered in burst empire, on the other hand a war-singed nation of five million. But the writerly traditions are deep in both Britain and Croatia. Dubrovnik's Marin Držić was making audiences laugh long before Ben Jonson's learned sock, and one of my favourite writers is Janko Leskovar who produced two short stories and ten novellas but then published nothing for the next forty-four years of his life.

Croatian Nights was born out of a shared fondness for hard drinking and a contempt for regular employment, but the contributors to this anthology haven't come together for a prose clash. The wordwatchers of Zagreb, the translators and adventurous publishers have generously and liberally purveyed British literature in Croatia, and the Brits here are grateful for the reception they've received. This anthology is a joint venture to celebrate the strong links between British and Croatian writers and the birth of what you might call Crit Lit. Happy reading.

Araby

Miljenko Jergović

God forbid you dream Ivan Zavišin's dream, people used to say even then. Or God save you from Ivan Zavišin's dream. And later, if a great and inexplicable misfortune overcame a person, it would be said that it was because of Ivan Zavišin's dream. In the end no one any longer knew who Ivan Zavišin was, or what the word dream really meant. But anyone who pronounced the word, aware of that instant when the tongue trills between 'd' and 'm', and the throat feels too narrow to express the vowel, knew full well when it was appropriate to summon the name of Ivan Zavišin and perform the little dance of sounds which can at first indicate misfortunes that need not be fatal, but which do not let a man rest until his dying day.

Ivan Zavišin was the last living member of a wealthy Primošten family whose crest may still be seen on the façades of the town houses they once owned, but which are today largely roofless. Blackberry bushes grow in the former drawing rooms, cats chase one another through the bedrooms and every February they howl and wail, so that on moonless nights the people think they hear the spirits of the houses' dead owners. The Zavišins' grandfathers are crying for help under hideous Turkish torture, the voices of galley slaves in Venetian ships are heard, while water pours into the belly of the ship and they rattle the chains that fettered them once and held them for ever, the Zavišins' grandmothers, high-class witches, burn at the stake, the bones of servants who mixed vinegar and wine crack, newborn bastards roll down stairs and heaven knows what else comes into people's heads on the nights when the cats howl.

There are five such houses, each one equally dilapidated because there were fewer and fewer Zavišins from generation to generation, but the houses were never sold. It was shameful to sell, because the only people who sold were the poor. But the Zavišins were always rich, and they preferred their roofs to collapse and a world to grow up in the ruins which would make the whole town tremble when the clouds covered the moon in February, and the cats began their feast of love. After Ivan's father died, followed by his uncle and aunt, two more houses began to crumble. People waited for the day when two more roofs would collapse and the wealth of the Zavišins would be reduced to the last house, the smallest of them all, where Ivan lived alone, because he had never married.

People came from Zadar and Šibenik to buy as long as there was still something to buy; he would receive them, entertain them and hear them out, but as soon as they told him how much they were offering, Ivan Zavišin would say that there was money enough for two lifetimes yet, and if they could somehow arrange that St Peter grant him them, he would give them the houses for nothing. The people would just look at one another and leave without saying goodbye. After the buyers stopped calling at his home, Ivan grew from a local eccentric into a dangerous idiot who was to be avoided. Although he never so much as looked aggressively at anyone, let alone did anyone any harm, it was enough for people to hear the howling of the cats in the ruins, those voices of the ghosts of the Zavišins, for them to shrink from the very idea of being in Ivan's thoughts. They believed that he was looking for a way of coming by those two lives he needed in order to spend the last of the family fortune.

At the time when no one wanted to hear about Ivan Zavišin

any more, and when people had already begun to take roundabout paths, just so as not to pass his house, the five ruins and the two which had yet to become that, and when his name would not be mentioned even in the most innocent conversations, at that time on the island of Sušak a woman gave birth to a son and named him Aladdin in accordance with her husband's wish. No such name had ever been heard in these parts, but no one was surprised by it. Sailors brought all kinds of curiosities home, sabres from Damascus, narghiles from Cairo, sextants from Manila, all kinds of diseases from everywhere, so why not a name. And the priest who christened the child said that it was pointless to register his name in the church books as Karlo, if the mother and father were going to call him something else. And in any case at the Day of Judgement we would not be recognised by our earthly names, but by the clay from which we were fashioned.

Forty days after Aladdin's birth, his father unexpectedly appeared at home. I've killed a man, he said, and I had to flee from my ship. They are bound to be looking for me and they are bound to find me if I do not run far away. Just let me see my son: if he does not remember me let my mark stay with him.

Beside the boy's pillow he left a Finnish knife. Its blade gleamed brightly in the light of the petrol lamp so that it appeared that the three lighthouses from the Cape of Good Hope had been lit in the poor little house. He did not see the tears on his wife's cheeks. Because he did not even look at her. He just gazed at the baby, trying to make out in his face its adult lines, the ones that determine similarities between father and son, but he found none, because those lines appear at the time when a human child begins to remember. And a lot of time would have to pass before then.

He left disappointed because he had not left his mark on Aladdin. Or that is how it seemed.

The mother put the knife away on top of the dresser, so that the child would not take a liking to it when he grew a little older. She was not worried about the blade, she would probably have used it to illuminate the house had she lived alone, but she was overcome by black forebodings because of the three lines cut into the rosewood handle. Her man had not killed once only, but twice more as well, with pleasure and the desire not to forget. He must have had another knife with which to record the crimes of the first, and heaven forbid that there were corpses marked on that one as well.

She knew that he would never return and she wanted not to remember him any more. She resolved not to speak to the child about his father.

But in vain: as soon as he began to speak Aladdin could already pronounce his father's name. My daddy is a sailor, he said at the time he was still wetting his pants. He was still toddling uncertainly round the courtyard when he knew the names of islands in the North Sea. Even that would not have been unusual if Aladdin could have heard these things from someone. But neither she, nor anyone else, had told him his father's name, nor could he have known that he was a sailor. His mother knew the names of the islands because once long ago, when she still believed in the blessing of their marriage, she had learned them from her husband on winter nights without candles or petrol lamps. The boy knew that, without being told.

She thought that maybe she talked in her sleep. So that the misfortune might not continue to grow, and so that Aladdin should not inherit his father's evil ways through her agency, every night before she went to sleep she put a raw potato in her mouth, and tied it in place with a scarf so as not to spit it out. In that way she was certain she would not say anything she should not.

Where's the knife? Aladdin asked one day. At that moment she felt icy hail crumbling under each of her vertebrae. There's no knife, she said. What do you mean? said Aladdin in surprise. My father left it for me. Haven't you kept it?

There was no anger in his eyes. He looked like a disappointed child who wasn't even going to cry. He never cried. He was calm, quiet and obedient, in every way better than the other island children. Nothing about him gave any cause for anxiety, apart from the names of the islands in the North Sea. His mother climbed on to a chair and took down the Finnish knife. Aladdin took a rag and wiped the blade. A beautiful knife, he said. You can open live shells with it.

The following day he tried just that. A short cry was heard, like that of a seagull, or a woman slipping in front of a cistern, and then he appeared in the doorway with his hand cut. From the root of his index finger stretched a diagonal gash out of which blood was spurting. As though he had tried to correct his lifeline. His mother wrapped his hand in cloths, and tied one tightly round his upper arm, but the blood would not stop. That's the Finnish knife for you, she said, trying to encourage his tears. These would make it easier for her. He did not cry.

Help me, people, my child's dying – his mother sped through the village. The people ran into their houses, the women lowered their eyes, the men rowed out towards the open sea. It was not good to be near when a child died. The young soul is tough and it can easily happen at the moment of death that it moves into someone else's body. And then there is a battle which is usually called madness. Two souls struggle over one body, but as it is impossible to throw the original incumbent out, for, however weak, it is in its own nest, so with the mad person both souls usually die or depart, and the grief ought to be double. Usually it is not like that, which only goes to show that those who are left on earth do not care so much for the lost soul as they are frightened that there will no longer be the body to which they have become accustomed. But that is a different story, important here only for it to be clear why the people ran away from Aladdin's mother. It would have been different if she had said only that the child had cut his hand and the blood would not stop.

As it was, the only people who wanted to help were three foreigners whose little boat with one sail had been anchored in the harbour for ten days now. They spoke some strange language which seemed to the ear at fifty paces to be pure Venetian; five or six paces closer it would have been understood by anyone who could get by in Spanish, at twenty paces it was pure Sicilian, while when a person was right beside them he would no longer understand anything, it was like having all the languages of Babylon in his ear. That is why the locals said that they had come from Araby, because no one had ever heard Arabian, and their clothing was such that it seemed they came from places where no Dalmatian foot had ever trodden. They were wrapped in black robes that reminded one of priests, but they differed from those vestments in that they reached to the ground and one could not see how they were ever taken off because their collars, without a single button, clung close to the neck. There was just one slit for the right arm, while the left one was always hidden. Whatever they did, on the boat or off it, they did with one hand, so that it seemed they did not even have a left one.

They followed the mother to the house. One brought fishing line, finer than hair or the tiniest down on a child's fingers, another brought a needle. The third did not cease mumbling in his incomprehensible language. She would say something to him, while he nodded his head importantly and carried on. He obviously understood everything.

While one held the boy's arm, the second sewed up his hand, and the third held the end of the thread between his index finger and thumb. Aladdin was calm and shook himself like a dog sheltering from rain only when the thread had to be pulled tight after the last stitch.

As they left, instead of payment the mother offered them a piece of bread. They did not take it, but she knew Venetian and had she stood fifty paces from them she would have understood that the black people would call again.

Araby

Ivan Zavišin had never set foot on a boat, or entered the sea. He had never in his life put so much as a finger into the water, to test whether it really was salty and whether the stones under the water were as smooth as people said, and whether crabs' claws were dangerous. In his childhood he had been forbidden to go close to the shore and that was the only prohibition he experienced from his father and mother. But it was also the only obvious mark of the nobility of the Zavišins. Never to step on to a boat deck, never to go down to the sea, never to look at, let alone touch, a net or a hook. The sea was the penance of the nameless poor, while to those through whom all the glories of the town's past were remembered, not one but at least seven pasts, it was given to live beside the sea and never notice it. When the south wind blew and the scent of the sea spread through Primošten, the Zavišins' stomachs heaved. That was also a mark of nobility. In his childhood, Ivan had simulated that nausea and imitated the adults who on those days cast from them all that they had eaten, and when he was himself grown up he could not stop his stomach heaving at the scent of the sea.

The islands were for the Zavišins what the stars and other heavenly bodies were for other people. Places of inscrutable longing and mystery in which the human imagination most likes to dwell and where the bright side of the soul travels every night. If it were possible to leap across the sea, or if a man were given wings, paradise would vanish. The poor would reach the stars, while those of noble birth would go to the islands. That longing was simultaneously so strong and so blind that it rendered invisible all those who had perhaps come from the stars, just as the Zavišins never met a single islander. And had they by some chance ever entered into conversation with such a person, it is hardly likely that they would have believed he had come from an island.

After people stopped entering the street with the ruins, the palaces that would become ruins and the house where Ivan Zavišin lived, he began gradually to become unused to people. At first he would still greet the villagers from the interior, when they brought him lamb, cheese, potatoes and salt, but then he began leaving them a ducat under the doorstep. Every Friday, they would lift the stone, take the gold coin and leave the goods in front of the door. They would ring the cowbell twice, Ivan would wait five minutes for them to be gone, and then take in the supplies. That was best. When you do not see human eyes or hear speech for long enough, you begin to imagine that they do not exist and that this world is made only for you. There is no better way of achieving immortality. When all other people disappear, your death loses its reason.

While the three black men were sewing up Aladdin's hand, Ivan Zavišin was already certain that he was alone in the world. And before dawn on the night when the black men crept into the little stone house where the woman was sleeping with a potato in her mouth and a scarf round it, Ivan Zavišin had firmly resolved to forget human language.

Three arms carried her out, quietly so as not to wake the boy, while she watched them with her black eyes wide open, unable to cry out, or move. Her arms hung down like the dead branches of pine trees broken by a storm, which had not yet managed to dry out.

The boy woke up alone. Outside he was greeted by human glances, which he could not recognise. The good and pious looked at him with contempt and withdrew before him into their houses. Those whom he had already heard cursing God looked at him with hatred, folding their arms over their chests or thrusting their hands into their pockets, kneading their balls and taking care not to prick themselves on any fish hooks. And those who were supposed to take care that those two worlds, the one that believed and the one that swore, should live in peace and harmony shouted that the whore had run off with the Arabians, leaving her bastard to them. Bitches leave shit outside the homes of decent people and hunters from Šibenik would have to be paid to chase them off and clean up the island. Fear the day when the church will stink of rotten fish, because there will not be enough incense. That's what they shouted, and the next day Aladdin sneaked into a trawler, dug himself in among the mackerel, seaweed and lobsters, and fled from the island.

All he took with him was the Finnish knife. And he resolved to find his father. He did not know what he wanted more: to save his mother from the black men and return home with her or to get even with the people, the good and those who were not, but particularly with the guardians of earthly and heavenly peace.

When he leapt out with the unsheathed knife, covered in fish scales, with seaweed hair and seven crabs which had grabbed hold of his flesh in their death throes, the fishermen thought that the Devil himself stood before them. Or at least the Devil's apprentice in charge of fishermen's affairs. They did not manage even to cross themselves, and Aladdin was already running over the foreshore, emitting cries that made even the stunned fisher folk feel like closing their eyes for ever at the horrors of this world. The ones they knew, but also those they had yet to live through.

Aladdin believed that the world was not much larger than Sušak, but he found himself in Primošten, which was more enormous not only than the world, but even than what could be imagined in dreams, which always seems far larger and broader than everything seen by the waking eye. But where was the North Sea and where were the islands, where was Araby where the black men had taken his mother, where was everything he knew, without knowing how?

He ran through the town for as long as his legs would carry him; people fled from him and he fled from them. He clutched the knife in his painful hand, because he knew that he could not appear before his father without it – when at last he found him. In the end all he wanted was to rest, but wherever he turned people who feared him would scuttle away. Finally he found himself in a deserted street, among ruins, in front of a house whose doors seemed long since closed.

He lay down under the porch, laid his head on the threshold and put the knife down beside him. Its blade gave off light until the sun went down, and then Aladdin was swallowed by darkness.

That was Ivan Zavišin's last night. After that night all that would belong to him was the time he spent awake.

Before dawn he woke with a start and rushed down the stairs. He did not manage even to put on his shoes, or to wrap something round himself, or to think about what was driving him downstairs. He unlocked all three locks on the door, burst outside, stumbled and fell. His head spun when he knocked the tip of his chin against the stone with which the porch was paved. The white light of the moon turned to red; it seemed to Ivan that the stone was burning. His legs buckled again. He turned as he lay there and found himself face to face with the boy. He was looking at him in surprise, and smelling terribly of fish and the sea. Ivan barely managed not to be sick; he grimaced at him, that was easier than speaking, but the boy stared back with the same surprised look. That was when Ivan Zavišin first thought that those were dead eyes looking at him.

He sat with his back turned to Aladdin and tried to think what he should do. But in his head there was a wall composed of irrational feeling, a thought that kept recurring however hard he tried to escape it – that he had woken too late and ought to have come earlier, while the boy was still alive. He felt guilty, but he did not know why.

It was already day when he finally stood up, laid his hand on the brow that was not yet quite cold and, with his thumb and middle finger, closed the boy's eyes. He caught sight of the knife, more beautiful than any he had ever seen. He picked it up, but there was not a single drop of blood on the blade. So the boy had not been killed. No one would bear his death on their soul.

He buried the body in the oldest of the five ruins, his great-uncle's house which had collapsed more than fifty years before, and for a long time he wondered whether to place the knife beside the boy. But he realised that this would be wrong. If he could not be buried like other people, and he could not because then Ivan Zavišin would have had to talk to the locals and explain what had happened, so it was better that he should not be buried with his knife, like a murderer. He also wondered whether he ought perhaps to break his silence because of the dead boy, but who would listen to him if everyone thought him mad and damned.

But perhaps Ivan Zavišin would have done that, if he had only known what would happen to him the following night.

He already knew that the dream was not his own. He was huddled in front of strange palaces, calling his father. He looked towards the sea, at the line where the sky began, because he knew that he was beyond it. So he fell asleep, called out in his sleep and dreamed again that he was in front of strange palaces, calling his father. As long as he did not wake, Ivan sank from one dream into another, constantly dreaming the same, always someone else's dream.

That was the first night, and who knows how many nights passed before the town learned of the torment of the man who spoke to no one, and whom nobody saw, because for a long time no human foot had stepped into the street with the ruins, the two houses that would become ruins and the one in which the last Zavišin nobleman lived. And nor would it until Ivan died in his sleep, until the last roofs also collapsed and every stone from which the houses were built turned to dust. By then the boat with the black men would have reached Araby, and people in trouble would repeat: God protect you from Ivan Zavišin's dream. And their throats would always tighten before their tongues uttered the sounds.

Hawaii

Vladimir Arsenijević

The evening was drawing in rapidly. It was Sunday. Their last day together. Martin had baked bread. Vera had made cabbage salad. A minute before putting the loaf in the oven, Martin had mixed a handful of roughly chopped almonds into the risen dough. Vera had dressed the salad with nutmeg, white grapes straight from the fridge and the juice of a lemon.

'This is a fantastic salad,' Martin acknowledged, with his mouth full, somewhat later, when they were sitting at the dining-room table. 'The paprika makes it hot, the icy grapes make it cold and neutrally sweet, the cabbage makes it sharp and the lemon juice makes it tart. I presume that it would be excellent also with a dash of olive oil and some crumbled ewe's cheese. You didn't salt it on purpose?'

Vera responded with just a nod. She was busy. Her whole jaw was occupied with gnawing at the almondy crust of Martin's bread, with its still-steaming centre.

'It's a shame I never made you pumpernickel,' Martin sighed. 'Then you would know what bread is. But I do admire your salads. I think that's mostly what I'll remember you by…' Although he was afraid that this would sound inordinately caustic, his voice surprised him by trembling with love and longing.

'Hmm, yes,' was all Vera was able to utter, still chewing and swallowing, determined to ignore the sudden flame in his eye. 'I suppose it's an innate talent. I only grasped the full range of my abilities at the time I was living with Jim in Honolulu. But I've told you about that, haven't I?'

Martin shook his head silently and brusquely. The flame in his eye vanished, and the warmth in his throat suddenly withdrew.

'Well, anyway,' Vera went on, paying no attention to anything, 'once it happened that we didn't have much food in the house: oranges, a mango, some pineapple and spring onions, that was roughly it. There was nothing for it but for me to put everything together in a heap, chop it all up and mix it with, I think, thyme and salt and pepper and lemon juice. Then I tried it and concluded that something was a little too strong compared to the other ingredients, so I went on chopping and adding this and that, whatever I had to hand. And I kept trying it. When the salad was finally ready, it had some white wine, vodka and a bit of sherry in it as well, and it was all in a plastic bucket. By then I was full and completely drunk, but Jim came back from the university ravenous. He ate three or four platefuls, I think. Then he was stuffed and drunk, like me. But still, before he collapsed and fell asleep, he concluded that the salad was perfect.'

Martin poured her some more beer in silence and she drank a long draught thoughtfully.

'The next evening – interesting the way I remember all this so clearly – I made him an even crazier mixture, with peanuts and brazil nuts, and the evening after that with eggs and bacon, then with mushrooms and basil. Then I went to the Chinese market and bought things that I thought were OK. I had never seen plants like that before, I hadn't a clue what they were called, let alone how they were used. I just asked the shop assistant, a Chinese man, whether they could be eaten raw without a person poisoning himself, and if he understood my question at all and answered in the affirmative, I bought them. And it all sounded like Dao Ping-

Pei or Kim Il-Sung to me. But Martin, what a salad that was, you can't imagine!' In her enthusiasm, Vera choked on a mouthful that flew straight through her mouth into her gullet, and stopped there. It was only when she had recovered from her coughing fit that she added, in a voice that was still broken and weak: 'Unfortunately, it has the disadvantage that it can only be made on Oahu. But I'd have nothing against seasoning it with prunes, rose petals or typewriter ribbon.'

Martin put down his plate and opened his third beer of the evening. Contrary to his expectations, Vera's story had put him in a good mood – in principle, he didn't like any of her stories that had any connection with Jim. 'Explore the unknown and use up leftovers!' He proudly proclaimed his own culinary motto, holding it to be an absolute truth, which Vera's story had only confirmed. 'That's the whole point!'

Wiping the foam from her mouth with her tongue, Vera relaxed contentedly, drawing her left foot under her right thigh. She took a half-empty pack of Silk Cut out of her pocket and lit a cigarette. 'Where was I?' she wondered. 'Ah yes! Then I made him pasta salad with mozzarella and lime and crushed ice and that night Jim screwed me better than ever before… You don't mind my saying that?… And the next day, when he came home, he just asked: "What are we having?" I brought out a crazy salad of celery, cooked artichoke hearts, Parma ham, chicken breasts, capers and raw mushrooms. The very next day I made him a hearty Mimoza salad, that's with cooked carrots and turnip and young beans and potatoes and peas, all with mayonnaise, hard-boiled egg yolks, crumbled whites, parsley and truffles, and Jim simply sighed' – she giggled – 'and looked at me besottedly.'

'I entirely understand.' Martin sighed too, completely enchanted by now.

'Then a salad of yellow and green peppers and smoked salmon and peeled tomatoes and stuffed olives, all covered in aspic, then pears filled with soft cheese with ginger and finely chopped walnuts, or extravagant miscellanies such as a salad of spinach, avocado and ham, or melon with prawns, things like that. Still, it seemed that Jim preferred simpler combinations: let's say slices of celery and radishes with double cream... And when I just think of beetroot – what wonders I created with beetroot, and chicory, and all the combinations with rice! I used to go to bed feverish – I would wake up devising the next day's mixture. I bought all the books about salads that could be found in Honolulu, I wanted to be a perfect housewife, I cared about making Jim happy. I was still so young then. I mean: how could I have begun to suppose that it was all beginning to get on his nerves!'

Draining his fourth beer, Martin moved closer to her and put his hand on her knee. 'It's not your fault. In Germany there's an expression for it: "A straw fire burns quickly".'

Vera sighed and was thoughtful for a few moments. 'Yes, it's true.' She smiled. 'Jim really was a balloon that went flat too quickly.'

And she looked Martin straight in the eye. She smiled and glittered.

'A balloon!' exclaimed Martin suddenly, and, as though there were a fire somewhere, he leapt up from his chair. 'A balloon! Hey, Vera, I've just thought of something! Look, as you're leaving tomorrow, and as I understand your definitive decision, I'm sure that I owe you something! Come on... here...' He held out his hand. 'I'll show you how to make a balloon out of a bin bag!'

Completely drunk by now, swaying as they walked, they went out into the back yard of the semi-detached rented pseudo-Victorian house at the very end of Grange Road in Ilford. Martin looked doubtfully at the leaden sky. Vera couldn't stop talking. But either he didn't hear her or he simply felt that there was no reason whatever to deign to respond. Resolved to devote himself for the time being to more important things, he spent some time just roaming around with a concentrated expression, collecting the material he would need for making the balloon. He went into the house several times and came back with various objects in his hands, and when he had put everything in a heap, he examined each item in turn attentively. Finally he turned to her: 'Pass me that tray over there, *bitte*!' he said, and the hard, German intonation with which he pronounced his order rang strangely in Vera's ears.

With an uncertain movement, she handed him the round container of thick silver foil where there had once been a frozen quiche Lorraine. Taking a scalpel out of his back pocket, Martin began to carve the tin, and soon all that was left of it was a cross-shaped construction, with a round rim and an opening in the very centre. Then he let the scalpel fall on to the thick, uncut grass and instead picked up a bright blue bin bag with the inscription KEEP BRITAIN TIDY. 'Can you help me?' he asked, in a considerably softer voice.

Together, they pulled the bag over the frame. Vera held it upright, while Martin used sticky tape to ensure that it would fit over the rim of the transformed container. He soaked a little ball of cotton wool in petrol and pressed it into the opening of the foil container. Then he stood up and considered his work with satisfaction.

'*Voilà!*' he said, in his comic French, '*c'est notre ballon!*'

Vera couldn't help laughing. She was genuinely excited, despite herself. 'Shall we let it go straight away?' she asked, tying her hair in a ponytail.

'No reason why not,' replied Martin, striking a Zippo lighter self-importantly.

Vera held the bag so that the flame, flaring immediately in the little ball of cotton, would not go out, and it began to swell rapidly in her hands.

Martin did not take his eyes off the bag, and when it was

completely taut he exclaimed: 'Now!'

Trembling, Vera let the balloon go.

The blue cupola just puckered and hesitated for a while, swallowing air and gathering energy. But once the balloon had finally separated itself from the earth, it continued to rise ever more confidently and swiftly towards the blue vault of the sky. For an instant, admittedly, it shrank into itself, and Vera thought that the flame would catch it and send it back in the form of black rain, but instead it increased its speed, swelled again and blazed, then sailed off into the distance, gleaming, towards the night sky of Ilford.

Something like a miracle occurred in the firmament. The clouds that had been dense until a moment before were suddenly rent apart, opening up a view of the infinitely dark sky. The balloon seemed to be sailing straight towards that rift. And down below, far below, in just one of many neglected gardens divided from the railway by a brutal concrete wall, Martin and Vera, two foreigners, living together in Ilford by several quirks of fate, rejoiced.

That was their last night together. The following morning, Vera would leave and they would no longer be a couple; after a year of living together, two years of going out and three years of friendship, they would part and nothing would be as it was before. They drank beer, stared into the sky and laughed excitedly. The moment was faultless – everything was being extinguished before their eyes, while they revelled in the garden, gazing at the roofs and the railway and the balloon that was fluttering its way towards the dark sky and getting smaller until finally it became just a bluish glimmer in the distance. Then Vera felt Martin's hand on her hip, but she did not stir. She leaned her head on his shoulder. The trimming on Martin's shirt smelled of flour.

Dear sir or madam,
I never believed in flying saucers. I believed, and I admit this, in flying
glasses and vases, but that has to do with the experience of a fairly intense

marriage from which I only recently, and, I'm afraid, too late, extracted myself, thanks to the blessed institution of divorce. However, be that as it may: last night (25.07.1993) I was sitting, knitting, as I usually do in the evening hours, when, suddenly, something transparent and domed hovered past my window. Towards the bottom of this unusual object, which emitted a blue light, I could clearly see the way the white rocket flame was burning. Completely flabbergasted, I dropped my needles and rushed out on to the terrace, but all I could still see was a little light travelling away at an incredible speed. I consider it my duty to bring this strange phenomenon to the attention of the local authorities, and the wider public!

Maria Koslowski

Nowhere End, Ilford, Essex

'It's raining,' said Martin in a hoarse voice, still breathing heavily, after he had glanced through the window in the hope of seeing the blue balloon somewhere in the sky. It was nowhere to be seen. The wind and rain would have finished it off – that thought made him sad.

It was nearly three o'clock in the morning. They were lying naked on the bed, smoking. Their last sex had been painfully practised, developing in an established way, like a ritual. Even the passion, which had undoubtedly caught them both up at a certain point, was connected exclusively with their shared sense that it was the end.

Turning his eyes from the window, Martin squinted absent-mindedly in the direction of a particularly lumpy spot in the surface of the red carpet and shuddered. 'Actually, maybe it's sensible that you're leaving.' He groaned, rubbing his face with his hands. 'London is a vile city.'

It had always amused Vera that Martin was so strongly affected by two insignificant things – the English weather and the English taste for floral patterns – but now, after everything, she was too sleepy to enjoy it. 'Presumably you don't imagine that Belgrade rain is any less depressing,' she responded, yawning. 'Or Belgrade wallpaper,' she added, smacking her lips and closing her eyes.

'I'm sure they're not,' replied Martin, gloomily. 'That's what's worrying me.'

'I'll come with you,' he said later, smoking in the darkness.

The rain was beating loudly on the window pane.

'Mmmmm,' said Vera.

'Don't go,' Martin whispered then, in a voice trembling heavily with nervousness and emotion. 'Don't go. Please, stay!'

'Don't be ridiculous, Martin,' replied Vera, quietly, almost inaudibly.

She could hear the tense burning of his cigarette.

'Then I think I'll go back to Berlin too, at least temporarily,' added Martin in a tone that for some reason sounded petulant, as though he were punishing himself with the prospect of Berlin, to spite her.

'Maybe that's not such a bad idea, Martin,' she replied, after a pause; she was no longer certain whether she was asleep or awake.

Martin's cigarette sizzled once more. Then he coughed. Vera felt that she was falling, losing herself, but she still heard him and understood when he said: 'Why wouldn't you come with me? We could have such a great time in Berlin!'

'Martin!' she responded, with her last ounce of strength. She wanted to add something, to say why that wasn't possible, but she was no longer capable of remembering what it was she should say. Someone was already calling something to her, from a distance, in a dream, and she hurried towards an intriguing new possibility, abandoning Martin without the slightest hesitation.

'I don't think it's at all sensible for you to be going to Yugoslavia, Vera. I understand everything – your mother is alone, and you have no choice. But can't you see what's going on there, for God's sake! You simply can't go there!' Martin flared, but it was no use: Vera was already sound asleep.

Waiting for a few moments for the whole jangling he had raised

to die down and be hushed, he slowly drew near to the sleeping
Vera, pulled the covers carefully and tenderly over her, kissed her
cheek and lay down beside her.

There were tears in his eyes when he said: 'Well, that seems to
be it.'

But nevertheless, the next morning, while Vera was getting ready to
leave, Martin rubbed his hands, scampered about, cheered her up
with his rapid babbling, a touching, friendly smile on his face the
whole time. He made her breakfast and coffee, and helped her to
pack. And when at the end he brought out a packed cake, which he
had secretly baked just for her, Vera was clearly and painfully aware
that it would take her a long time to erase him completely from her
system, he had got so deeply under her skin, and how good it was,
how brilliant it was, fantastic, that she was going for good!

'Honey, almonds, cinnamon, coffee, ginger.' Martin murmured
just some of the ingredients of his cake, knowing that Vera did not
need details.

'Thank you!' she said, hugging him and kissing him, for the last
time.

At that, fairly amusingly, he collapsed straight into the armchair
that happened to be behind him. But nevertheless, the chair whined
painfully beneath him. Suddenly, his face darkened again. 'I don't
know how I'll live without you,' he muttered, from the armchair,
turning his face away.

Vera sighed deeply. It annoyed her that he was starting again.
She didn't know how to explain everything to him. She didn't
know whether there was any point in explaining anything. So she
replied: 'You'll get used to it,' with a fairly cold smile. 'But, Martin,
look: I really have to go now, but I've remembered that I owe you
something as well, before I leave,' she added, looking at her watch.

For all his fifty-two years, Martin was really a child. In an
instant, just as she expected, Vera had his full, alert attention.

'Yes,' she went on, 'you remember you once asked me to show you my favourite children's game, only I couldn't decide? Well, I think I now know which it is. I'll demonstrate, OK?'

Martin was ready to agree to anything at that moment, and when, leaning over him, she held out her hand with such self-confidence and from such a great height, he had no choice but to grasp it.

'Stand up, then,' she said, softly. 'Stand here. Not there – here,' she ordered, giving him a gentle shove. 'There, that's it. And now, raise your arms. Good.' Coming up behind him, she stepped out of his field of vision and put her arms firmly around him. Her breath was excitingly sweet; it tickled the sparse golden fuzz on Martin's neck and his spine tingled. 'Are you afraid?' she asked him then, in a whisper.

'No, no.' He smacked his lips nervously. He didn't know what was in store for him, Vera was quite certain of that, but he added bravely: 'Just carry on!'

Well, you should be, she thought of whispering, but she restrained herself.

'Just a brief introduction,' she said, instead. 'We used to do this as kids just about every day, I think. Several times in succession. What I want to say is that it looks dangerous, but in fact it isn't: it's great! So, someone comes up to you from behind, just like me now, and grasps you – like this.' Vera pressed herself up against Martin's back and placed her fists on his chest. 'Then you have to breathe, as deeply as you can, ten times. When you breathe in for the tenth time, you hold your breath and close your eyes. OK?'

'OK, baby,' Martin confirmed.

'Good. Come on, then – breathe deeply. That's it. As deeply as possible. I'm counting: one … two … feel free to close your eyes … four … breathe deeply, Martin, no slacking, you'll see what you missed out on in your childhood just by being born in Germany … seven … I used to be able to do this so expertly, I wonder whether

I'll remember after all these years... nine... and... ten! Now, hold your breath, Martin!'

As she uttered the last sentence, Vera screwed up her eyes and thumped her joined fists violently, like a hammer, straight into Martin's diaphragm. His body leapt up of its own accord and before he had managed to work out what was happening he was floating high up, like the blue balloon, everything around him was swirling and spinning round, he could just still hear the rain beating persistently down on Ilford, but even that sound was becoming blurred and disappearing, 'Ah, ah!' he said, sinking into a mass of colours and sounds, 'Iloveyoumartin,' he heard Vera's voice shot through with celestial resonance, he wanted to smile at her, he wanted to kiss her, he wanted to hold her back, but he could not see her: something had devoured the image before his horrified eyes and she had broken up into a million little greenish-blue squares...

He couldn't see anything any more apart from the whole infinity of darkness and silence through which the blue balloon with the inscription KEEP BRITAIN TIDY was floating freely and joyfully.

And when he came to, Vera was no longer there.

Dear sirs,
Last night I was standing gazing out of the window of my cell, it could not have been more than 10 p.m. Greenwich Mean Time, and thinking about the sermon I had intended for next Sunday, entitled 'Save us, oh Jesus, from temptation and hellfire' (and at the same time, at least up to a point, I was praying for inspiration, because for some time now I've noticed that my flock is conspicuously somnolent on Sunday mornings), when from the other side of the not exactly gleaming window pane I caught sight of an unusual phenomenon: very visible against the dark firmament of the heavens, some kind of bluish object was floating under the dense clouds straight towards me. When, borne by the winds, it had come sufficiently

close, I realised that it was not a matter of any kind of 'object' but of the unambiguous apparition of the translucently blue-white figure of the most holy mother, the Virgin Mary. However, what astonished me most was the discovery that her golden halo was not in its usual place, but, on the contrary, somewhere at the level of the feet of the blessed Mother of God, which, to make the whole thing still more mystical, were clothed in a pair of the most fashionable silver sandals! That experience led me to the firm conviction that all the representations of the Virgin Mary, in which she was consistently portrayed with a golden halo round or above her head, were thoroughly wrong. The golden halo, I can confirm, is in the region of her feet! Nodding to me benignly, the apparition vanished before I was able to recover from my shock. I immediately changed the title of my sermon to 'The apparition of the Virgin Mary with a golden halo at her feet – a reminder of the humility one should show towards one's neighbour, even if he is a filthy foreigner'.

The Right Reverend Padraig O'Neill,
Church of Saint Mary,
Harold and Maude Road,
London

Split

Niall Griffiths

About two hours into the journey from Zagreb, and bored, he asked the group of lively young men sitting next to him on the back seat of the coach whether they spoke English and they said yes and so he began talking to them, fine and friendly fellows all. Three hours or so into the journey from Zagreb one of them cracked open a bottle of brandy which they told him was made from 'grass' and five hours into the journey they swapped football shirts; his pristine new Vodafone shirt (he was from Richmond upon Thames, who else was he going to support but Manchester United?) for their slightly creased and whiffy Dinamo one. He put it on over his T-shirt; a perfect fit. Six and a half hours into the journey the young men disembarked at a small town and waved him off from the bus-station bar, and seven hours into the journey he was drunker than he could ever remember being, the grass brandy howling through his skull like a wind, and eight hours after he left Zagreb he got off the bus at Split, staggered a bit off the bottom step with his legs all brandy-bandy and moved, unsteady and foreign and tendentious, towards the sea.

Split, then; he's in Split. Drunk and alone in Split. One of his lecturers back at Warwick University on the 'Palimpsest City: Expeditious Utilisation of What Already Exists' lecture course had told him that the Dalmatian city of Split was the finest example of

compact and stratified architectural styles in Europe, if not the world, so he'd applied for a grant, failed, got the money from his parents instead, and with that had made the journey to Croatia – plane to Zagreb then coach on to Split. Spend some of the summer here in this ancient and fascinating and beautiful port, is what they said he should do, but they didn't tell him about the uncommon strength of the grass brandy nor the exuberance and thirst of the Croats in drinking it nor even about the *jugo* wind, this horrible, warm, wet waft that slaps his face and sets his teeth grinding as he looks out at the sea with the sun sinking into it behind the island and then turns and regards the colossal mountains that hem the city like a vast splashback and the strange people grumbling and growling around him as the force of the sticky wind pushes their lips back up over their long teeth. It reminds him of the only time he visited Wales, at Barmouth: the snarling people and the sea in front and the mountains behind. He felt trapped then and he feels trapped now. Except here in Dalmatia he can't just jump on the next train home.

He reels over to a bench and sits down, plonks down, frightening a gull which rises above him screaming like an irate sprite. Brandy-heavy fingers dig in the side flap of his rucksack for his hotel reservation information; the Hotel Marjan, and a number. Now where might the Hotel Marjan be? He turns on his mobile and waits in vain for a signal then tuts and turns it off again and staggers up on to the prom, the embankment where only a few scattered and harassed people brave the *jugo*, which snaps awnings and thickly whistles through empty chairs and tables outside the restaurants and bars. Lost utterly, he feels, but he'll ask someone; ask them politely whether they speak English and then ask directions to the Hotel Marjan. That's what civilised, social, educated people do, and he's *English*, for God's sake; he's all of those things. He may be somewhat crapulent but no amount of alcohol could ever completely obliterate his singular carriage, his dignified bearing.

Niall Griffiths

There's a group of young men on benches over the road, doing what young men everywhere do of an evening to kill time. Behind them is a mural on a limestone-block wall; a football, a flag and the words HAJDUK ŽIVIVJEČNO. Ah, a football – a chance, then, to show some solidarity, to re-find himself and where he is through the international lingua franca of football. He removes his jacket to reveal the shirt given to him on the bus; see this, look, I like Croatian football too. We can be friends, can't we? Just give me directions.

'Excuse me, lads…'

Good God, that brandy; his own voice slops in his ears like porridge. Their heads turns towards him and it seems he can hear the grinding of their necks as if rusted metal moves on metal. They have strange eyes.

Panic could arise here. He can feel his tongue and his chest wanting to be frantic.

'I'm sorry to bother you, I…'

One of the young men stands up. Much bigger than he seemed when seated.

'Do any of you speak English?'

The big man smirks and holds his finger and thumb an inch apart: 'A *leetle*.'

'Ah, quality, quality. Now we're getting somewhere. I, ah, I'm new in town and I appear to be lost. I wonder if you could…'

Something is going wrong here. Now all of the young men are circling him and their eyes are darting between his own eyes and the crest on his football jersey and he can now hear their breathing mingling with the whine of the wind and he can see flared nostrils and gums. Oh, they have strange eyes, these foreign people. Like scallies all over the world.

'Sorry, I'm lost, I'm a fool, I…'

'*Znam*.'

'Pardon?'

That voice, rumbling. He heard voices like that and saw faces like that a few years ago on the TV alongside images of villages in red and eager flame.

'*ZNAM.*'

Said with anger. And of course, he thinks, these people are Slavs – they're warlike, wild, lawless. He may be in some trouble here.

A finger prods his chest.

'Now look, mate, I'm an architecture student from England and I would like to …'

'*Baš me briga.*'

Others repeat the phrase: '*Baš me briga!*'

'No no, I don't speak your language, I'm English… please, I only know English …'

A big finger prods his chest again, harder, right on the crest over his thumping heart, and the hot wind licks across his face like the tongue of a leech, bringing to the surface of his skin his rapid blood and his confusion and fear and isolation. He is alone here, alone and English among this bellicose race, these Croats, these people who even astonished the SS. The only thing he can possibly do is run.

So he does. Pursued by bedlam in a strange and shouting tongue, he legs it back down along the embankment towards a tall illuminated tower above the roofs, some possible sanctuary, past the ranked tables at which no drinkers sit and through the wind like warm treacle and left into an alleyway and down through cellars where the coolness clutches him instantly, and panting between stones increasingly irregular of surface and of edge, as if he scarpers breathless and afraid through time, through history itself. This is what he travelled all that distance to see, this tangible march of the world, the progression of Europe through the stones of Split city. He didn't come here to have it all blur past him as he flees from some Slavic scallies. What's he done to annoy them? He's English, and he's not a football hooligan, so why are they so intent on his pain? What on earth has he done? He's done nowt!

NOTHING!

He stops to listen; yelling and pounding feet, bedlam bedlam bedlam. He darts through a dark entrance into a high round room, ill lit and shadowy, the starlit sky above as if this is a huge chimney, a cooling tower or something like that. He manages to stop running an instant before crashing into a fat bearded man with black bog-brush eyebrows being dressed in a ceremonial gold-trimmed white robe by two thin and mincing lackeys holding pins in their pursed and lisping lips. The fat man looks at him, one of those bushy eyebrows raised inquisitively.

'Oh.'

'"Oh" indeed,' the fat man says.

'Who are you?'

'Who am I?' The fat man snorts. His voice is ridiculously posh; he sounds like Brian Sewell, Leslie Phillips and the Queen all rolled into one. 'Who am I, you say? Strange little man. I, sir, am the Emperor Diocletian, and as I am about to address my public I alas have no time for banter so would gladly thank you to get to buggery and vanish. And if you've come into the vestibule to relieve yourself like so many of your plebeian ilk are wont to do then I would request, nay demand, that you take your business elsewhere as the place has become a midden. A midden, sir. You stand in a site of high grace and culture and I will not tolerate any disrespect. Now piss orf.'

One of the lackeys pulls the robe tight around the distended belly and the emperor says 'oof' and cuffs him around the head with a fat hand wrapped in a thick gold chain like Ali G. Our man hears running feet behind him so shoves the fat emperor out of his way and bursts through another door and runs across a square where watery shapes around him could be either phantoms or just wind-coaxed tears and he leaves that square and runs down a narrow alleyway barely shoulder wide – this strange and ancient warren of a city – and into a wider space, marble flagstones under foot, where what looks like a monastery or priory or something like that lies derelict and covered in graffiti, some in English, the names of forgotten eighties punk bands along with political slogans and swastikas. Surely he can't get any more lost. Aimless, he runs through space, time, self; see the dark shapes here he didn't know existed, see the emotions and judgements he has corralled and fenced off. See the soul he has from the very first breath Balkanised and ruled. *Divide et impera.* The warring tribes of him now unwarring under his own *pax Albion*, yet neglected they still and always seethe.

He stops, gasping. Hears laughter and chanting and sees a group of monks, brown robes, sandals and tonsures and large crucifixes, dragging a coffin from the cathedral between some black sphinxes. On the flank of one is a yellow graffito: BOOTS N BRACES. One of the monks trips and stumbles and the coffin falls and skids and bursts open and bones spill. A skull rolls and stops and leers.

Oh God, that brandy. This wind. This *place*. What's going on here?

Over his shoulder, down the alleyway, comes noise again; bedlam bedlam bedlam. So he runs again.

He just runs; across a small square that he assumes must be a fish market because of the stinking linger and down thin alleyways and through portals and under roofs and also under the ground through cool vaults that echo back his heavy breaths and the swift beat of his feet and past holes and chasms which emit dark rays like anti-lanterns, some of these places still unexplored, unknown and secret, as if they could ever be anything truly but. He runs past palm trees and shoe shops everywhere, he's never seen so many shoe shops in one place before, and he runs under loggias and vestibules and peristyles vaulted with cupolas and he runs through tricliniums. He leaps over a piscina and through a caldarium and also through an exedra and he skirts a huge hole at one side of which is another square, this one crumbling, dilapidated, once-walls now mounds of beige blocks like empty cardboard boxes behind a warehouse. There is a rumbling high in the sky as of some propellers and that rumbling quickly heightens and tightens and becomes a scream, a shriek growing louder, unearthly and demonic and enraged, and he knows what it is, in the lowest reaches of his stomach he recognises the sound: a dive-bombing Stuka. He's heard it on old films.

'Oh Jesus Christ! What's happening to me! I'm from England, this shouldn't be happening to me! Oh God! Mum! Dad! Help!'

He dives behind a wall as the bombs burst instant red and skull-cracking. Shrapnel spits and fizzes and a hot fist whacks him. Another whine begins high among the stars and he runs over to some people looking static and fish-eyed down into the crater which has revealed more Roman rooms, more chambers, and these people ignore him as he shakes them and points to the wailing sky and tells them that they are being attacked. These people have junkie eyes and junkie skin and junkie hair like most of the people he encountered on his day-return to Glasgow and one of them manages to muster a laugh as another bomb bursts and both hot stone and steel shrapnel fly through his torso as if he has no more substance than a ghost.

And what does our man do, our English student of architecture? Well, he legs it yet again, down these labyrinths, now streets, running breathless, mind awhirl, through a tramping Roman legion which ignores him completely and past another bloody shoe shop, and his pursuers may have ceased or may not but that has stopped being the point. He just runs. He's English and that's what he does, flees from it all across Carrara Square where a young man on a scooter proffers a handful of white pills to him and past yet another shoe shop (ooh, nice pair of trainers in there) and under a huge gate and up some steps and past a giant statue of a robed and bearded man holding a book, a big gold shiny toe on this figure which he stops to rub as he passes without any idea why. He sees a church tower standing alone, then he sees it as part of a church and then he sees it surrounded by smoking rubble and standing alone again and someone who could be either Mussolini or Alexei Sayle cruises past in a long, low thirties-style open-top car and stops and beckons him over. He approaches. Benito or Alexei stands, folds his arms across his barrel chest, and booms in a Brummie accent:

'Thowse who foind it convenient to forget their histor-ay will foind themselves condemned to repeat it, loike.' He thinks for a moment then says: 'Or somethin' loike that, anywye. Moiks me cowin' sick.'

Alexei or Il Duce drives on and our architect-in-training resumes running, around the church tower and back into the sticky wind and around a corner and into a crowd of creeping people in berets and waistcoats and clogs, all carrying guns. He yelps scared and surprised and spins to flee in the opposite direction and one of these men shouts:

'Ey, lad! Seen that fat fuckeh Mussolini anywer, av yeh?'

Oh no! Scousers too! With guns! Run! Run from this brandy-madness and wind-sickness, this insane crazy place, this bad-dream city which contains the world racked and stacked up above his head and around him, run through it all and from it all until every sign of it has gone. Run to the sea and then just swim away, and he hears a tinkling, a faint sound of splashing water, and he runs towards that noise down another alleyway and past, yes, yet another shoe shop, these people here must walk a lot or else secretly be centipedes. Towards the sound of water he goes, maybe a river or a stream or a branch of the sea itself, but no, it's none of those things, it's a waist-high bronze teacup on the pavement at the foot of a wall and twelve feet up on that wall is a clenched metal fist from which gushes an arc of water down into the waiting teacup. Preposterous sculpture. Pointless. Daft. There is nothing going on here that he feels it necessary to know about.

And this place to him is much too strange. Unfathomable it is, here, in this low city of incessant destruction and rebuilding, of stanchion from the ash, of bomb and massacre turned to seed. And of the wind, which has blown his skin to sandpaper, so he leans into the bronze teacup to rinse his face in it, in the water from the fist, and beneath his own startled reflection is a jumbled human skeleton, the skull of which grins at him just as the monk-spilled one earlier did and which wears around one of its wrist bones a thick gold chain, and he looks up unwashed away from the bones in the water and sees a sign below the spurting fist that reads BORN TO BE HAPPY and he runs away from that, runs again, sluggish now and tired, too tired to be frightened, down on to the promenade where he sees an iron fishhook about ten feet high embedded in the harbour wall. He imagines the size of the fish they must catch here, the same size as the coach that brought him from Zagreb, and exhausted now he leans back against that hook, his chest heaving, and his eyes slip slowly closed. He hears triumphant shouting in the city in front of him and intent splashing in the sea behind. Either the Croats will get him or the monster fish will and he really doesn't care which; either way, the buried and segregated parts of him are going to be rent asunder, separated, split. Liberated, perhaps. All he knows is that he's sick of running and he wants it all to end. He's English. He's a foreigner. It's not what he does.

Storm

Ben Richards

'January, February, March, AYP-RIL, May, June, July.'
The big bartender raised his bushy eyebrows at me; his fists were clenched tightly. I smiled politely, cleared my throat and then sang tentatively.

'January, February, March, AYP-RIL, May, June, July.'

He threw his head back and shouted a laugh while a gold crucifix danced on his Adam's apple. Then he grabbed the bottle of homemade liquor that he had told me was called biscuit and poured us both another large shot. His hands were huge.

'I really don't think…' I began. The barman put his fingers to his lips and gestured to the glass. Drink. We both downed the shot in one. I felt the hot burn of alcohol, the faint suggestion of wild herbs. The bartender's eyes glistened. There was neither good nor bad humour in them; he reminded me of my cat Blackburn after it had caught a fly and was batting the dazed insect along the floor.

'August, September, October, November, December,' he suddenly roared as he got up, in a shuffling dance that made me think nervously of the ear guy in *Reservoir Dogs*.

Who wrote this stupid song and why was the bartender so obsessed with it? I wondered through a fog of alcohol. But more importantly, how had I ended up drinking with this psycho in an otherwise empty bar in the Istrian seaside town of Rovinj?

*

Things had started badly when Gemma realised – with her usual exemplary timing – that she had run out of Tampax just as we were about to arrive at the beach.

'We have to go back into town,' she said.

I sighed. It was hot and I could see the sunlight on the sea. We had just come all the way from the centre of the town. My thighs were chafing slightly, the kind of pain that can easily transform itself from minor irritant into soul-destroying agony. Why hadn't Gemma remembered the fucking tampons while we were still in town? Typical, typical, typical, I hate you, why am I with you, I wish I had never met you.

'If it's a problem I'll go on my own,' she said. 'I'll bring us back some ice creams.'

'Yeah, it would really make my holiday if you got abducted by some psycho Croatian truck driver and he drove you out to some remote farmhouse and raped you and then buried you in a box and I was stuck here with no idea where you were.'

''Cos that's so gonna happen,' she said, taking my hand as a couple of kids walked past with their own ice creams and a three-legged dog stopped to sniff our feet.

We trekked back into town where every building appeared to be flying a Croatian flag. I hate demonstrations of national pride and found this one particularly irritating. There was also a distinct lack of chemists or even a supermarket in Rovinj. In fact, there didn't seem to be anything in this seaside resort apart from cafés, restaurants, shops selling rubber dinghies, bats and balls, cheap sunglasses and postcards of girls with bouncing breasts.

'Go in there.' Gemma pointed to one of the tourist shops. 'And ask if they sell Tampax.'

''Cos that's so gonna happen,' I replied.

Finally, we went into the tourist office.

Storm

'Could you tell me where we might find a chemist?' I asked the pretty, sulky girl behind the counter. She spoke only Italian and German, which was no good to us at all. Then the phone rang and, to my fury, instead of answering me she answered the phone. Her face lit up in a smile. It was clearly a personal phone call, a boyfriend from the way she started fiddling with a kiss curl.

'This may be the new number-one holiday destination,' I muttered to Gemma, who was standing on one foot, 'but the idea of service is wholly alien to them.'

I was still smarting from the previous day in a café when a hatchet-faced waitress had spilled a bottle of Coke over Gemma and then not only failed to replace it but also kept it on the bill. OK, I could understand them not wanting to cater to the whims of dumb tourists who hadn't bothered to bring a spare Tampax, but if they were stupid enough to fight a war for even more borders, if they wanted capitalism, then they were just going to have to adjust to all its brutal exigencies.

Employee of the month put the phone down and stared at us as if amazed that we were still there. I thought Gemma might be about to cry, and when we finally managed to convey the urgency of the situation, the girl softened and gave her one of her own Tampax. While Gemma went to the toilet, I asked her about all the flags in the town.

'Storm,' she replied, as if we had asked for a weather forecast.

I gave her my best you-are-a-total-moron stare. There wasn't a cloud in the sky.

Gemma and I had another small argument on the way back to the beach. She wanted to buy some of those weird rubber jelly shoes in case the beach was pebbly. 'You buy some too,' she said in her usual bossy way. I told her I didn't want any but she insisted. 'Go on,' she said, 'they only cost two pence.' I was suddenly struck with a very precise image of where I would rather be than Rovinj at that moment. I wanted to be in my living room with a cup of proper tea on a day of cloud backlit by pale sun, the suggestion of later rain, my cat Blackburn hanging purring on my shoulder, Bob Dylan on the stereo singing 'Absolutely Sweet Marie', my computer screen showing the little red message 'You've got e-mail'. Not buying the beach shoes became almost a reverse categorical imperative for me. I would never give in; I would swim out to sea or drink hemlock rather than buy those stupid shoes. I told Gemma this and she rolled her eyes, called me a boring, self-obsessed misanthrope, and bought herself a pair. Then she dawdled for ten years around an ice cream stall.

'Do you think,' I asked her, applying sarcasm with the biggest spade I could summon, 'that some time today we might get to dip our toes in the Adriatic?' I had to walk slightly bow-legged to stop my thighs chafing. I needed to lose weight. 'Fat cunt,' I said to myself. 'Fat, hot, useless cunt.'

Well, anybody can be just like me - obviously…

Gemma changed her mind from chocolate to pistachio and then asked me in a facetious tone how to say raspberry in Serbo-Croat.

But then again not too many can be like you – FORTUNATELY.

'You!'

'What?'

'Now you. Sing.'

It was obvious he was going to put me in his truck, rape me and bury me alive in a box unless I humoured him. I was very drunk now, having consumed at least ten beers and half a bottle of the mistletoe-flavoured lighter fuel that the bartender had pulled from under the counter with a triumphant smile. At the time I thought he was just glad to have a customer. Now I realised he was toying with me before tying me up and rolling me out of the back door to his truck. All the Croats I had ever met – not, admittedly, many – drank in this weird way. It was all good-natured bonhomie to start with but it wasn't long before cute Mogwai turned into deranged Gremlin.

The bartender was gripping my arm and muttering something about an island. I couldn't make out its name but it sounded something like Brian.

'February 2 1905. James Joyce. Birthday. In Pula, yes, but also went to the island. Mosquitoes all gone – petroleum. Nice Nobel Prize for Robert Koch. We drink some more beer. And Nehru and Nasser and Sophia Loren. And zebras and antelopes. Ho Chi Minh. All gone now, all gone…'

He poured another drink and downed it. Then he wiped his mouth. I was in Croatia listening to a madman talking gibberish about zebras on the island of Brian. About as much fun as reading *Ulysses* with the added promise of being buried alive at the end of it. I had to get out of there. I tried to get up but he put his hand on mine.

'Sing!'

I looked at his clenched fists again.

'OK, erm, August, October, November, October, Decemberrrr…'

I tried to get up again but he pushed me down.

'You forgot September. I speak English better than you. Listen.'

He enunciated carefully, wagging his finger to each month.

'August, September, October, November, Decembeerrr.'

He poured another drink for us both.

'Now you.'

'August, October, November…'

He banged his fist on the table.

'No! You forget September. Remember September. It is important.'

Of course it is, of course it is. I was about to start crying. Oh, where are you, Gemma, why did I run away from you in the seaside resort of Rovinj? Choose any flavour you want, take all the time in the world, I'll shower Tampax upon you and wear jelly shoes for the rest of my life, but where are you now, where are you tonight…

'Go on, jump, you big girl.'

The beach in Rovinj should have been closed down for even daring to use the term. Pebbles would have been a luxury. The so-called beach was really a coastline, a cruel landscape of giant rocks, and you had to jump off them to get in the sea. Gemma floated in the delicious-looking clear water below me, having whisked off her clothes and leapt in with the criminal abandon that she had probably learned in her girl's boarding school along with midnight feasts and muff-diving. Or midnight muff-diving. I wanted to jump because the water was so inviting but it was too high and I wasn't sure – especially with the surplus weight I was carrying – that I might not descend further than her, break my legs and drown. Next to Gemma, a middle-aged German was floating on his back, smiling encouragingly at me. Alongside them an unmistakably gay Mexican had taken off his swimming trunks and was laughing and waving them at his friends on the shore. The German conformed to genetic imperative and decided that my impending leap was somehow his business.

'Come on, it's easy. You jump, *ja*, it is perfectly safe.'

Yeah, like I'd believe that from a *German*.

'Oh, I know, thank you, I'm not scared. I'm just looking for the right place to jump.'

The German and the gay Mexican both burst out laughing and the German turned to Gemma, who was floating serenely on her back, long red hair fanned out on the water like the Lady of Shalott.

'If he is not scared then vy are his legs shaking so?' And the Mexican laughed and swallowed water.

At least I'm ENGLISH. At least I'm STRAIGHT.

I jumped.

'Yaaaayyy.' Gemma doggy-paddled up to me. 'Isn't it lovely?'

Storm

And it was lovely. I turned on my back, looking up at the clear blue sky and thinking with derision about the idiot tourist woman who had predicted a storm. Then I got bored and decided to get out again to read my book, and that's when all my troubles began.

How to get out?

'It's easy, look.' Gemma swam up to the rocks, waited for the swell to lift her a little and then scrabbled up to safety.

But she was wearing jelly shoes. So was Hitler, so was *Y tu mama también*, so were the kids we had seen earlier eating ice cream, so was everybody in the sea apart from me.

Gemma held her nose and dive-bombed back into the sea, splashing me.

'See?'

I couldn't mention the shoes as that would give her an unbearable sense of self-righteousness. I drifted up to the rocks and felt the dangerous, brute power of the swell. Then I closed my eyes and half drifted, half hurled myself at the rocks, scrabbling like crazy, falling back, just getting a foothold. I would be dashed to death, there was an undertow, I would be sucked under the rocks, I had to escape, swept up again, I made one last effort and scraped myself on to the rock.

A delta of red scratches covered my white stomach. My fingernails were sore and, when I looked down, my feet were lacerated, cut to ribbons. I took a few agonised steps, then turned shaking my head to reassure Gemma that – while shocked and in pain – I was basically OK.

They were all laughing.

The. Final. Straw.

I think behind me I could hear somebody shouting. Come back. Where are you going? Please, Reuben. Don't be silly. But there were tears blinding my eyes. I hated holidays, I hadn't wanted to get a Ryan Air flight to Trieste at 4.30 in the morning, I was doing fine at home, I was safe in the living room, I was too fat, my thighs were chafed, my feet were bleeding, the Croats had no idea of the service culture that modern capitalism demands, people lied and said there was going to be a storm when there clearly wasn't, everybody else could get in and out of the sea in their tuppenny plastic shoes, I was being laughed at by a German, I had to use Internet cafés to access my e-mail, I was missing my cat.

I grabbed my clothes, pulled them on and headed towards town, propelled by a full tank of fury. The Little Mermaid knew nothing about pain compared to me but I was too angry and upset to care. I stormed past streets of rubber dinghies and buckets and spades. The girl from the tourist office was chatting outside to some preening Italian who was admiring his own body more than hers. She smiled and nodded at me as I went past but I ignored her.

A cold beer.

And then work out how to get rid of my so-called girlfriend.

Quisling.

A cold beer and a cigarette.

Sobriety is all very well but then why bother living?

I would rent a one-bedroom flat with a small but practical kitchen in which I would drink moderately, cook frugally and entertain a different girl every week.

But first a cold beer and rest for my damaged feet.

I wanted to find a bar without a national symbol hanging from it. The excess of red check flags was making me feel nauseous. Then, down a small side street, I saw exactly what I was looking for. No flags, just a battered, run-down old bar without even a name and one white plastic table and skew-whiff parasol outside. A wonderfully lazy and grudging admission that this might be a bar. My only worry was that it was so authentic that it would be full of gypsy types spitting on to the floor or Croatian skinheads who might mistake me for one of their many ethnic enemies, but, to my delight, there was nobody sitting on the battered red plastic seats inside. There was only a very large bartender in a shirt open almost to the waist with a gold crucifix around his neck…

I didn't think the bartender was going to rape and kill me any longer. First, he was too drunk to tie a knot, let alone drive a truck or dig a shallow grave. Second, he was weeping. He had gone back to the bar for another bottle of biscuit and also some photographs. In one of the photographs, the barman was standing grinning, holding a rifle. Another man and a woman who looked incredibly like Gina Lollobrigida accompanied him. In the other photograph, the barman was with the same man as before but this time they were also with a Chinese man. All three men were wearing panama hats.

'Ho Chi Minh,' the barman said, and I laughed because the man did look a bit like Ho Chi Minh.

'Who's the other guy?' I asked.

The barman gave me a baleful, lachrymose stare.

'August, September, October, November, December,' he intoned, and showed me a photo of a zebra and some antelopes which he claimed were on the island of Brian off the Istrian coast.

'Right,' I said, glancing nervously at the door, and there, better than six white horses arriving at the penitentiary, was Gemma and – traitor as she was – I have never been so relieved to see anybody in my life.

'Oh, Reuben,' she said. 'I've been round every bar in Rovinj. I was so worried about you.'

She looked at the bottle of spirit we were drinking.

'Biska,' she said, 'is fucking lethal.'

'Lethal.' The barman smiled happily as if it were the finest adjective in the world. 'Tonight we kill ourselves.'

'Well, he just might.' Gemma nodded at me. 'You were doing so well and I was so proud of you.'

'Shobriety,' I said wisely, 'is all very well. But what's the point in going on living?'

Gemma stared at me for a second and then burst into tears.

Ben Richards

I glanced at the beer bottles, the overflowing ashtrays, the empty and half-filled bottles of biscuit. I was going to have to start all over again.

The barman sat Gemma down and poured her some biscuit which she accepted with a resigned shrug. She wrinkled her nose as she drank it and I remembered that I didn't hate her. The barman patted her head and told me I was very lucky to have such a beautiful girlfriend. And Gemma finally dried her eyes and picked up one of the photos.

'That's Gina Lollobrigida.' She sniffed.

'It looks like her,' I agreed. 'This was *apparently* taken on an island called Brian off the Istrian coast…' I hoped our host wouldn't pick up on the light sarcasm.

'Brioni,' Gemma said. 'I read about it. It had a safari park and lots of famous people used to go there before… well, you know.'

She stared hard at the photo.

'This *is* Gina Lollobrigida.' She looked at the other photo and turned to the barman, her rings flashing in the dim light of the bar. 'And this is *you*, look how handsome you are, and oh, wow, this other guy must be Ti… '

'January, February, March, AYP-RIL, May, June, July,' the barman sang.

Gemma looked at him steadily.

'OK,' she said. 'Sure.'

I glanced at them. They were both mad but I thought I probably wouldn't move into my new flat as soon as I got home. There are some things you can't forgive but Gemma hadn't known how bad my feet were when she laughed with the German. I would have to show her later and then she would understand and I would make her laugh by pretending to walk like the Little Mermaid.

'He forget September,' the barman told Gemma.

'He forgets a lot of things,' she said.

I could see this was going to develop – yet again – into one of those scenarios where Gemma was going to be more popular than me.

'Why haven't you got a flag?' I asked the barman.

He looked puzzled and then he nodded and muttered 'Storm' a little grumpily.

'There's not going to be a storm,' I snapped, but Gemma put her hand on my arm.

'Operation Storm,' she said quickly. 'I read about it in the guide. It was a big victory in the war when the Croats retook the city of Knin from the Serbs.'

The barman must have heard the word Knin because he snorted contemptuously as if retaking Knin were tantamount to conquering Hull.

'What's in Knin?' I asked.

'Flags,' said the barman. 'Many flags.'

He poured us some more drink and stared at the photos of Gina Lollobrigida and Ho Chi Minh. He looked so sad and so far from the deranged rapist I had first imagined that I was desperate to cheer him up. So I stood up and roared.

'August, SEPTEMBER, October, November, Decembeeerrr.'

And the barman and Gemma applauded, and the dropping sun suddenly filled the bar entrance and I could just see the sea glittering through the open door and smell fresh fish frying. Perhaps I could try to make an effort, I thought, as a drowsy cat which looked a little like Blackburn, although obviously not nearly so pretty or well looked after, wandered into the bar. And the cat sat down and started scratching the street dust from its ear while staring at me through deadpan amber eyes, as if it were watching over me.

Gobbledegook

Tony White

'Maybe you should write some of this down?'

She didn't sound that sure of the idea herself, but was still surprised by the vehemence of his answer.

'No! I've written *enough* about it all. *Too damned much*. You wouldn't believe it.'

Blimey!

'I'll *say* anything you want, over some drinks…' Was he flirting with her? '…but I'm not going to write it down. Not going to bloody *sign it*.'

Wobbly, unshaven – he was talking quickly. Bright eyes looking at something behind her. The dark fan of soot up the wall where the flue went in behind the stove.

'What would I write about anyway? The whole lot? It'd be a bloody book.' He struck a poetic-heroic pose, hand on heart: 'In the early morning light the very *mountains* seemed to be clothed in the rough, grey-brown uniforms of the Serbian army. Their…'

She laughed – couldn't help it.

'God, I could write all that easily enough. And I wouldn't spare you the gory details either. Doesn't take much to get a confession out of me. Always think it'll work out if I just… *confess*! Get it all down. Two-finger typing in the middle of the night then going to bed in the early nip of morning. Waking up to cold stewed tea and the nostalgic tug of England. Reaching for the cigarettes and finding the tin under a pile of crossings-out. Jesus! Problem is once they're there in black and white you're stuffed, aren't you? Got a life of their own. God, I should know. I'm the past master! Write it down? No one ever had to wring it out of me, I bloody volunteered it. Didn't just sign my confessions, I refined them, edited them – read and reread them. Signed them "Lots of love" then *posted* the damn things.'

The quick gust of laughter didn't break his darkly pensive expression.

'Or might as well have done. Let's face it: you can't camp next to the metaphorical fucking pillar box every time, can you? Beg the postman to give it back: "Terrible mistake. So sorry. Would you mind awfully?" Once you've written them you might as well have sent them, and once you've done that they're gone. Off in the world, wreaking havoc.'

Who's gone? she thought to herself. *It's not the letters that have gone, is it? What was he saying last time?*

'You were saying. You said that you'd lost touch with one of your contacts?'

'Did I? Oh, yes. More than just a contact, I'm afraid.'

'I'd wondered. Do you think that she was captured? Killed?'

'No, no, no. Ran away. Forged in the heat of war and all that... Buried the poor girl under a heap of troth. Always bloody plighting it. Can't say I blame her. Frightened her off, I suppose. Chose the wrong way to impress her.'

'How did you find out?'

He looked up quickly, then away. 'On bloody duty, wasn't I. Crouching in the attic, notebook on lap, as per usual.'

'Did she use the broadcasts? How is the message passed – I'm assuming your network had their own system?'

'Poems. The message is... We'd put the message in the tenth line.'

'So...?'

'Came in and I thought, This is bloody familiar, then there it bloody well was. "I shall flee to other shores." She knew I'd get the reference; that was our song. It's from "T'ga za Jug" – "Longing for the South" – sentimental sods, aren't they? Not a bloody peep since. Not a dicky bird. Of course, I'd guessed already, I suppose.'

'You both came up through Salonika?'

'Of course. But there's a bit more history than that.'

'Did you think about…'

'What? Jacking all this in and going to "other shores" myself?' He stopped for a second, a sour, disdainful expression on his face. 'Not very specific, is it. Not much to go on! I could always write a postcard, I suppose, poste restante other bloody shores! "Arriving on the eleven o'clock from Beograd!" Sorry, I don't mean to be sarcastic. It's not your fault. Not sure I feel like talking about *that*, actually. Her. Not today. Do you mind?'

'Is that when things got more… difficult?'

So she did mind, but the question was ignored. He'd been sharpening the pencil as he spoke. He took it out and inspected the point, then put the sharpener down and fiddled with the ruled pad that had been on the table since the beginning of the session – closing one eye and lining it up so that its bottom edge ran parallel to the table-edge.

'You were saying that you've written a lot.'

'Oh, God! Haven't we all? I mean: reports, letters, transcriptions, *encryptions*, *zar ne*? I still feel like I'm wearing those bloody headphones now. But Christ, I couldn't leave it be. Always doing it the hard way. One thing I've learned in life – and God knows I've learned this the hard way – is that when you are absolutely set on one single, final course of action and you've got to bloody well do it now and hang the consequences… That's the time to stop – let time take its course. Doing nothing is better. Doing *anything* else. Because whatever it is you're planning you can damn well guarantee it's the wrong thing.' He looked up – not at her, then at her – and said, 'Sorry, wandered off the point.'

While he was speaking he'd turned the pad forty-five degrees, anticlockwise, and started drawing. A line now zigzagged across the top of the page – a graph with no axes. Could be measuring anything. Reminded her of one in an old school geography book. 'Rainfall in Britain since Roman times'. But beneath the line he quickly sketched some diagonal downward strokes – not a graph. Mountains?

She said nothing. Stayed perfectly still – wanted him to forget she was there for a while. If that were possible.

What kind of a job is this? she sometimes thought to herself. String them along for a bit, poke them about to try to provoke some kind of reaction. And keep doing it until they're strong enough not to come any more. Then you can finally forget all about them. Keep their files in case something messy happens in a year or so… But it didn't do to think like that. This was supposed to be useful. Supposed to help. For God's sake, they always turned up, didn't they? Always polite, deferential. Even him. Never late. An hour or two of very politely talking to *himself* more than to her. Always said the same thing at the end of the sessions; habitual charm ran through him like the letters in a stick of rock. 'Thanks. Let's talk about you next time!' Then he'd grin sheepishly as if he'd just told a risqué joke at a dinner party.

Outside she could hear voices and footsteps. She thought of hot, dusty streets rather than mud; longed for summer to arrive. He was still sketching. Seemed little point in stopping him. The sun. A valley, a jagged ridge. It was like a child's drawing. Rocks strewn across the valley floor. A puff of smoke, then another and another. Little matchstick soldiers moving across the landscape like ants. Some climbing up to a V-shaped niche in the rock. Flower patterns. Intricate. A city. Shoebox skyscrapers with rows of square windows and big radio masts on top – all of them with big, ragged, smoking holes punched through the walls. Bombed trains. Broken bridges.

Doodlebugs in the air with dotted-line trajectories. Doodlebugs? Had the Luftwaffe used doodlebugs on Belgrade? Would have if they could, she supposed. They'd used everything else. A ditch piled up with matchstick corpses.

They both looked at it for a while, neither acknowledging the other's presence, until: 'These "outbursts", as you called them…?'

She was changing the subject. Trying to get something out of the last quarter of an hour. Didn't need to look directly at the clock these days. Not since she'd noticed its faint reflection in the window opposite. That had taken her the first few months of her posting – up until then she'd propped her watch beside the flower pot on the window sill, *just* where they couldn't see it. Otherwise it was no good at all; no matter how discreetly you peeped at it, they'd notice.

'What?'

'These "outbursts". Do you want to tell me a bit more about them?'

'Not much to tell – don't know too much about them myself, to tell the truth. Must be in a bit of a daydream or something. Can't remember what I'm saying, afterwards. Just moments in time – no before or after. But it's as if there are people looking. At me. I want to tell the truth but I can't. No, that's not it. A sense that I'm expected to tell the truth; no… that I'm expected *not* to tell the truth. So I don't. Only sometimes. Sometimes I do. Sometimes I have to. *These* times. And then I just blurt it out, but no one's paying attention to it. Except it's not "truth" that has any value – or any *sense* a lot of the time. Just things that I'm sure at the time feel like *demonstrable* truths… I don't know.'

'Are you aware of what you're saying? I mean, at the time. Are you telling these truths about yourself? Is it you, actually *you*, that's on trial?'

'No. I mean, I don't know. Not judging by what I seem to blurt out. From what people tell me. Nonsense a lot of it.

Gobbledegook. And it's in bloody Serbian apparently!'

'The people in the… dreams tell you this?'

'Tell me what?'

'That it's gobbledegook?'

'No, the people… the ones who bloody well sent me here. Chaps in the office. Well, I don't blame them; the typists were getting upset. They always put it so well. You know: "Look here, nothing to worry about, old man. Do you good to have a break. Nice girls over there – *lovely nurses*. Lucky sod – almost wish I was going myself!" Then they all breathe a huge, collective bloody sigh of relief as soon as you're out of the door. Done it myself. Methuen got referred here last year, didn't he? Can't have people upsetting everyone left, right and centre, can we. Not good for morale. Get someone dependable in. No, I mean, as I said, I've done it myself. Participated. Drawn corkscrews in the air when he wasn't looking. Rolled my eyes at my superiors. Thought he didn't notice, but I bloody noticed, I can tell you that for nothing. Poor Methuen was going through bloody hell, though, wasn't he? Pathetic, really. Sorry, I'm not… Oh, don't worry. I know you're not supposed to talk about it, but you know what I mean. Generally speaking. Slightest thing and he'd faint, or *feel* faint. No, that was it: convince himself he was *going* to feel faint then get himself all worked up and end up nearly fainting from the anxiety of waiting to faint. Sitting there sweating in silence, terrified that he might feel faint at some point in the future! A grown man! Afraid to stand up in case he fainted. Unable to stand up and speak at the same time, in case… Good God, I mean, you can laugh, can't you, but "Cup of tea?" doesn't work with people like that, does it?'

He looked at the drawing as if someone else had done it. Reined himself in. It took a few seconds.

'Listen to me. People like *that*. I mean people like me.'

Contrast, she thought to herself, making a mental note while pausing to let the insight sink in, or to mark it at least, *between lucidity and presentation of symptoms. Check frequency of episodes? Harbingers? 2-3-4.* Then she picked up the conversation again: 'Gobbledegook?'

'Sorry? Oh, yes, yes, so I gather. All sorts. Nonsense. Something about Labradors and Mr Nice, I don't know. Mr Nice is taking his Labradors to the opera. Something like that, ha-ha. That was one. So I'm told.'

She looked at the file which was open on her lap, leafed through a couple of pages and then read aloud from it: 'Um, "I can't use it since Mr Nice did not ask any questions about the opera case or Labrador."'

'Ah, yes. That was it, was it?'

'You don't remember?'

'No. 'Fraid not. Sorry.'

'That's what it says here. Seems pretty innocuous stuff when you see it like this, but you were quite distressed, I gather. Sobbing it out, over and over again. Can you remember why you feel so distressed? I mean, it happened again yesterday, Staff Nurse told me. In the canteen. Can you remember anything about that? She's not so good at writing these things down, so I don't know what you were saying.'

'I don't know either. Sorry. I'm not sure exactly.'

She looked at the file again. 'Someone's translated these. Here's another one – there are a few here. "I'm sorry this cord of my headphones is very short. I can't even stand upright. Sorry. It's fine now."'

She looked at him and raised her eyebrows. He shrugged.

'All sounds pretty meaningless now, doesn't it,' she went on. 'Not exactly gobbledegook, but it doesn't sound like something to get worked up about, does it? None of this rings any bells, I suppose?'

He shook his head apologetically.

'Can you remember at all what was so important about them?'

'Oh yes. Yes, I remember that all right.'

'What was it?'

'I told you. That they were the truth. *That I was telling the truth.*'

'Here's another one, "Operation Hedgehog" or something.'

He laughed quietly to himself. Shook his head. 'Operation Hedgehog!'

'And this wasn't an op you were familiar with?'

He hesitated for a second. Old habits.

'Listen, I might be a woman, but in this room I outrank you, you know. This wasn't an op…'

'No!' Laughing dismissively but good-naturedly. '*Hedgehog?* No. Nothing like that! We don't call things "Operation Hedgehog" in the SO, for God's sake!'

'There are various conditions, of course. Things we can rule out. Don't take this the wrong way. You've heard of Tourette's syndrome.'

'Uncontrollable outbursts, you mean. Profanities? Well, the outbursts I'll give you, but you're not…'

'No. No, of course not, but I'm interested in the difference.'

'Between what I… what I've *got*, and…'

'Tourette's, yes. Why not.'

'And what is the difference?'

'Oh, plenty. But the daydreams. Visions, whatever you want to call them…'

'I don't want to *call* them anything. I want them to bloody go away!'

'Hallucinations are more common than you'd think, in these situations. Though I'll admit that yours are slightly unusual – a bit more… complex, self-contained.'

'Thanks. I'll take that as a compliment.'

'You don't strike me as being shell-shocked. I mean, I can understand that you may feel a certain amount of guilt – we all do, don't we? Perhaps that's why you see yourself up against some kind of… *charge*. Maybe you're indicting yourself. Do you notice if there's anything special about the moments when these… episodes occur?'

'Well, it's not like there's a loud noise and I'm under the table *soiling myself*. Just suddenly, yes, I suppose there is some sort of feeling of guilt. I'm in the dock. But it's not *my* guilt. This all sounds potty, I know, but it's not like any court you'd get back home – nor over here for that matter.'

'In what way not like…'

'Crowded, very crowded. Like Nuremberg – you've seen the newsreels. But not like that, more like a radio studio – you know, white walls, microphones. And movie cameras. People everywhere looking at radar screens. Oscilloscopes. With *words* on them. People watching who I can't see. A vast bureaucracy. Like Babel – everyone talking different languages. Bosch and everything. Dutch. English. But I'm the only *Serb* – even though I know I'm not. And everyone's… looking at me, analysing every sodding move. Incredibly convoluted mind games. People trying to *second-guess my triple bluffs*. They sound pretty queer now, but those things I say… I feel I have to cling to them like bloody life-rafts, because they're more important than anything else. Because they're just plain, old, simple truths. What was that one you just read? "The cable on my headphones is too short," was that it? I mean… Just to say something, anything, *true* like that feels like such a damnable relief.'

'Do you think it's the newsreels that have, you know, planted this idea in your head? This image?'

'I don't know, but no, I don't think so. Not speaking in bloody German, am I, for one thing.'

'Your Serbian is good?'

'Of course. Wouldn't have got very far for King and bloody country otherwise!'

She decided to be blunt. It sometimes worked. 'So why are you there, in these dreams? Let's call them that.'

'Buggered if I know.'

'What did you do that was so terrible?'

He didn't answer for a while, then said, 'Nothing. Well, no more than any of us.'

They sat in silence for a few seconds, before there was a slight change in the pattern of her breathing. He'd not noticed the pattern of her breathing until it changed, but he recognised it now that it had. Remembered the code. If it weren't so slight he'd think her withdrawal of attention was almost ostentatious. But it worked; it was second nature now. Like the tenth line. Though he'd forget this immediately, until the next time; until the end of the next session.

'Ah. Time's up, is it?' Charming sod. Flashing the old smile now as if the past hour hadn't happened. She could have been someone he'd taken a shine to in the pub or on the bus. Something was certainly working all right. She could give the bugger that.

'I'm afraid so. See you again on Thursday.'

'Right you are!'

Standing up, he took his jacket from the chair-back and smiled. 'Well, thanks. Let's talk about *you* next time, eh? We should, you know, *idemo u kafanu* some time. If you fancied. You know where to find me.' He actually *winked* before he opened the door and stepped outside.

Shaking her head, she listened to his footsteps, his scuffing walk. She carefully tore the picture from her pad and slipped it into the file.

Relief

Borivoj Radaković

I'm sprawling comfortably in the shade, with my feet on the railing. Pero is sitting leaning his elbows on his knees. He's a bit subdued, he doesn't like heights. I always laugh when I remember him once saying that he likes height but only at a distance. But my ninth floor is quite normal for me. When I go down to someone on the fourth floor, I have the feeling that I would be able to step out of the window and take a walk, it's so low down. I'm on holiday, Pero hasn't had a job for the last ten years… I'd far rather sit with him, because we don't have to talk, and if I had gone to Crikvenica – no, I'm not going to think about that now. Mira is… no, I won't… It's summer… it's good that she and the little one have gone to the sea, they'll both have a good rest, and I'll have a good rest and get ready for the new school year. I mean, fuck the bloody headmaster and some parents: let the children do this, let the children do that – school's not a parliament, for God's sake! You daren't look a little sharply at a child these days, without its parent storming in: 'You're inhibiting my child!' And the little genius is already in the third year, and hardly knows how to write a single letter by hand! All they do is strum on a keyboard. Soon no one will be able to write any more.

I take a beer from the table. I look around. My Zagreb relaxes me. Maybe because the view is always the same. Apart from when

they dropped those two or three bombs. That column of smoke by
the theatre ... They were aiming at ballerinas, fucking bastards ... To
the left and right: buildings, high-rise; down below: the wood
around Bundek; opposite: the detached houses of Trnje; in the
distance the green of Zrinjevac, the cathedral, then Sljeme; then ...
Europe, then ... the sky; then ... maybe a black hole, why not? I
always maintained that information was eternal, everything is
eternal, nothing is lost, nothing is forgotten, you can't destroy
electrons. And electrons remember. For ever. And that guy's only
now changing his theory, what's his name, begins with H ... The
one in the wheelchair, um ... Oh, fuck it ... To the left, above the
Zagreb hills, there are a few clouds. They could come to
something. Please God. Here − I'm only sitting, but I'm dripping
with sweat. It's sultry. I put the bottle to my lips, but I hear Pero:

'What do you think, what's worse, having your tongue or your
eyelids cut off?'

I think it's a joke, so I laugh: 'Where the hell did that come
from ...?' but I see that he's quite serious.

'It doesn't matter, what's worse: no eyelids or no tongue?'

'No tongue of course!' I say without thinking, but I see him
screwing up his face, so I hurry to justify my position: 'Imagine
only saying: m-m-m ... your whole life.' I want to be witty too. I
mean, that's what you have to do with these has-been lads, you
joke, you swear ...

'And not being able to sleep your whole life?'

'I think ...' In fact I give up straight away. I don't feel like
thinking about it. And I don't think about the fact that there was
something hard, almost aggressive, in his tone. I'm feeling lazy. And
it's stifling. And outside nothing's stirring. Not a breath of air. Just
two or three cars on Freedom Bridge; everyone's left the city. I nod
my head towards Sljeme. 'It's going to rain.'

'When I was a kid I read about an Indian torture ...'

A bird flies past. A crow, or a rook, or something. Like the one the kids once caught behind the school. They pulled its wings off, the monsters. They were playing 'Animal Planet'! I don't think I've ever slapped anyone so hard as I did little Hodak. And I should have hit his father as well, then let the dad and his son complain that they were inhibited… This one's flying fast. I watch it go. I hear Pero moving. He's breaking the foil on a little card and shaking a few greenish pills on to his palm. His hands are shaking.

'What's that?'

'From the doctor.' He picks up a beer, takes a long swig.

'Listen, beer and pills don't really go together…'

He puts the bottle down on the table, still holding it with his outstretched hand. He makes a face, as though a pill has got stuck in his throat or he wants to throw up. I want to ask him why he's taking them, but I say:

'Bitter?'

'That's torture.'

'Pills?!'

'Bugger pills! No eyelids…!' He's frowning, his face contorted. 'I didn't sleep for nights because of that… Not now either… I don't sleep.' He looks up at me: 'A knife, then they take hold of your eyelid with their thumb and first finger, stretch it and snip! The skin's gone!' He shudders. 'Like circumcision!'

'What a comparison…!' and I wonder – where did *he* get the word 'circumcision' from? I want to tell him that I was in Montenegro some years ago, in Bar, and some guy was having his son circumcised and invited eight hundred guests, and everyone brought a gift of money, but he's carrying on, as though he's moved away somewhere else.

'Both the top and bottom lids. And blood is pouring into your eyes. You can't wipe them to save your life…' I imagine at once that I'm wearing a rough woollen jumper, and raise my arm to rub my eyes… 'And you can see everything around you. Try sleeping!' He looks at me as though I was arguing with him. 'And the sun's baking…! And the wind's blowing over your eyeballs, and dust is falling into your eyes, and flies, all kinds of shit sticks to them, thorns jab into the white of your eye, into…' His voice is increasingly hoarse. '…your cornea, into… your pupil, into your brain, into your fucking cunt. Into your marrow… I've been through all that…'

'In a dream, I'm glad to say…' I say, getting up, and I put a hand on his shoulder as I pass. 'I'm going for a pee.'

I didn't realise he was so emotional. It's obviously really got to him, but what can I do? I'm surprised he never mentioned it before. OK, we haven't met up for a while, although we live in the same apartment block – he on the second, me on the ninth. I invited him up here for a beer, nothing more, because… there's no one else around. And he's the best of men, we've known each other… for ever. We were at elementary school together. He didn't get on at school, but he got some sort of training. Honestly, the salt of the earth, he'll do anything for you. Fridge, toaster, short circuit, something needs to be carried – just give him a call, he'll fix it. He never takes money, it's got quite awkward. We're all like that, those of us who're left in the building, everyone knows something. I come off worst, fuck it: I write their funeral orations. I teach their children and I bury them. I always make the whole crowd weep, and they like that. I've already seen off six people in our block. When poor Marijan was killed on the Kupa, his was the first funeral I spoke at …

There's a spider in the corner by the toilet. Fuck it, if Mira was here… 'Go on, little one, enjoy yourself, we've got another ten days…' I've told her a hundred times – don't kill spiders! She says I'm superstitious. I'm not superstitious, but – let it be, for God's sake, it's alive, what have you got against it? My stream is stopping. I take a little piece of skin on my cock between my thumb and forefinger and rub it a bit. Then I take hold of my eyelid, and stretch that too. Identical! *Where* did he get that idea? Hey, are you

Borivoj Radaković

crazy? I say to myself. Sometimes he really surprises me. Like when he fucked with Jura…

'Hey, remember Jura…' I say when I get back to the balcony. He's staring straight in front of him. It's all quite black over Sljeme. 'I can't wait for it to rain.'

'The tongue's nothing.'

'Oh, that's enough!'

'Why won't you let me finish?'

'I'm not stopping you, but…'

'So why are you interrupting me? You always want everything your own way. That's what all the lads say. And you haven't a clue!'

What's he mean, 'all the lads'? Bugger him. I, with my teaching diploma, make no distinction between any of them, I mean, here I am with him, having a normal conversation. I'm not like Žac, or rather Dr Vidmar… strutting about, fuck it, he doesn't know anyone in the block any more. I look at Pero. Who the hell are you to tell me I haven't a clue…

'About what?'

'You haven't a clue what happens.'

'When?'

'When your eyelids are cut off.'

'Oh, fuck your eyelids!' I point to his bottle: 'Drink up and I'll bring some more, and stop going on about it…'

'There, you see, you're interrupting!'

I can't stop myself, but I stare straight at him, idiot that I am, and say: 'It hurts. It takes a genius to know that?'

'You see, you haven't a clue! First it stings, then it hurts…'

'Same bloody thing!'

'It's not the same bloody thing! It's all a process. First it stings.' How persistent he is, damn it. If he was always so systematic, he wouldn't keep being out of work. He can hold out only for a few days. A thought flashes into my mind: once, long ago, maybe in the eighth grade, I tore his jacket. Accidentally, we were kids, and I knew it was new, and they were poor. He cried. That bothered me for ages. Fuck it, I didn't mean to. Maybe he's getting his own back? Suddenly he hits me on the shoulder, startling me. 'Look!' He separates his upper and lower lids with the thumb and forefinger of both hands and stares at me. His eyes bulge, the whites are suddenly large, and in the centre the corneas are yellow – in fact for the first time in my life I see that he has yellow eyes – and as he stretches the lower lids downwards, they show their pink lining. He looks like an idiot, sad and stupid at the same time. 'And imagine if you were like this, not for a whole lifetime, for a week. That's enough… Try it, try it!' He doesn't move his hands. 'Go on!' Then he leans towards me: 'Well?'

'Oh, come on, the kids in my school do that.'

'*You* do it! Come on…!' and at that he kicks me on the shin under the table.

It's like an electric shock. All my nerves flare, my body jerks, my blood starts to race. He didn't kick me hard, but …

'What the fuck?'

He's still got that idiotic look – mad, innocent, dangerous. He doesn't seem to notice that I have completely lost it. Or he doesn't care. Or is that what he wants?

'Well?' he says.

I look at him. 'Is it because of your jacket?'

'Jacket? What jacket? What are you waiting for? Come on!' He kicks me under the table again.

'Wait, then!' Fuck you, what the hell are you thinking of! Suddenly I don't want to stop myself, I take a swig from the bottle, then bring it crashing down on to the table, close my eyes tight, then open them wide and lean towards him. 'There! What now?'

He leans his elbows on the table and stares at me.

I stare back at him. Like, who can hold out longer? Just look at him: he's not stirring. Just staring like a basset hound. In fact it's as though I am seeing him for the first time. In fact, he has no expres-

Borivoj Radaković

sion on his face at all. It's stupid – this could lead anywhere. OK.
We'll do it, and then we'll go down to the bar. I can't stand insistent
people. Besides, it's easier for him. The sun is lower in the west now,
and it's glaring underneath the cloud straight into my eyes. Well,
that's enough of that: I turn towards the city. I can sit like this for
three hours. Sljeme has already disappeared. It's going to be some
storm! I need to blink, but I won't. Out of spite! Bugger him. Since
he's driven me to it, then we'll keep going to the end! I move my
eyes rapidly from left to right. I can feel him still gawping wide
eyed at me. As though we're in a madhouse. And I've let myself get
drawn into this! I can cheat – how can he know whether I've just
blinked or not – only, what for? Besides, fuck it, it stings, it really
does sting.

'I've had enough.' I want to pick up my beer casually, but my
hands fly up of their own accord and I start rubbing my eyes.

'You see?' He's still holding his lids open. He says hoarsely, 'You
see how it stings?' His lips seem to be moving by themselves
between his hands. 'Afterwards it burns as though lasers were
boring straight into your eyes.' Only then does he lower his hands.
There are deep lines under both his eyes. He closes them tight, but
doesn't rub them, just shakes his head. He doesn't open them. Tears
squeeze out between his tightly closed lids and slip down his face.
He doesn't wipe them. I turn away from him, I can't look at him
like this... I feel uncomfortable, embarrassed. I hear him saying: 'It
doesn't hurt till later,' but in a muffled voice, he must be wiping his
eyes and face with something now. As though he is choking, or
really crying. But I still don't check. I don't like it when someone
dumps all their demons on my table. Fuck you, mate, we're not that
close, I'm not interested... But he carries on:

'Then your veins start exploding...' I glance at him again. He's
grimacing, as though his capillaries really were bursting. 'Then your
eyes dry out. Like dried figs... like crackling... like shit...'

'Come on, don't give me all this crap,' I say, standing up abruptly and collecting the bottles. I hear him getting up, shouting after me:

'There, you see, you won't give in!'

What the hell's got into him? We've only drunk a couple of beers... Unless he'd been drinking before he came up to my place. And who knows what sort of pills he's on. Maybe he can't stand the air pressure. The bio-meteorologists are right, it affects... But that's enough, no more funny stuff! We'll just drink this, then down we go to Toni's. I'll buy him one drink, and then I'm off. I don't like it when you're having a drink, and someone starts snivelling.

I chuck the empty bottles into the crate, take two new ones out of the fridge and go back to the balcony. To my surprise, Pero is standing by the railing, looking down. I leave the bottles on the table and go over to him to see what he's looking at. Nothing. Just then someone comes out of the building. Oh, I know her at once even from this height.

'Look, it's little Iva,' I say, and actually I want to make him think of guys' things to forget what we've been talking about. 'Dad's an idiot, but Mummy's ... Eh?'

Her mummy used to be a stewardess. She never came to parents' evenings, but she always caught me in the lift, like, listen, I know what your job's like, but I'm having a bad time, you know, my husband... A mobile rings. It's not mine. Her husband got several years in clink. Some hanky-panky, financial engineering. It rings again.

'Your mobile, Pero.'

'Eh?' As though he's on another planet, fuck it.

'Your mobile.' I point at his pocket. 'It's ringing.'

'Eh!' He takes out the phone. 'Hullo?'

Little Iva is already disappearing behind the block. She must be going out, to town. I used to give her nothing but top marks, because of her mummy. But now, not a word of thanks, she doesn't acknowledge me. She's a cheeky kid, she walks cheekily, her hair swings on her head. Sixteen. When I see her in the lift, those low-slung trousers, below the belly button, thin skin, taut ... fuck me if I won't lose it one day and run my hand over her flat little belly. It's unbearable! How do the boys manage with them? And I don't know what I'll do in two or three years' time, when my little one gets into that kind of thing ... Who can look at that? Her little tits have already begun. Like little Bibica Ban in the second row of desks. Maybe I should have gone with them to the sea, to begin getting used to it. That always gets me going, like now, I can feel it, my ears are burning, my cheeks are tingling, I run my hand over my forehead – I'm sweating.

It's hot as hell. It's hard to breathe, those cigarettes will kill me, bugger them with their cigarettes. When is it finally going to rain! It's already reached the Sava, it's overcast, clouds, leaden. There's no sun any more. This is the worst. And little Iva will get wet, Mummy's treasure. Or she'll scuttle into some fool's flat and have it off... She's bound to have long ago ...

'You don't know me,' I hear Pero say into the phone. I didn't even notice him sitting down. He's got his profile towards me, he's staring out into space. 'No one knows me.' He's nearly shouting now.

'Hang on a minute ...' I want to tell him to calm down, because the neighbours, the next-door balcony, they're the limit, you can't have the radio on remotely loudly without them calling and saying it's bothering them. Pero's looking at me, but he's saying into the phone:

'You don't know me, I tell you!'

A different man. Cracked up. Must be the pills. I have a mind to take the bottles back, but he picks his off the table and pulls at it. What on earth was I thinking of, bringing them...?

And what the hell was I thinking of, when we met in the lift, and I invited him to my place for a beer? What have we got in common, the fact that we went to school together – fuck school!

He's plastered, the slob, and he's drugged himself, and now… OK, it's better that he drinks it up and gets completely legless, then I can shove him into the lift. Just look at him! Boy, are you drunk, you idiot!

A violent gust of wind. All of a sudden. I turn round.

The storm!

Down in the little park, the trees are swaying wildly. The wind is howling. Cartons and plastic bags fly through the air. Just let the first drop fall, just let it start. It'll do this fool good as well. I look at the sky: get on with it!

And: it starts! The first drop bursts on the ledge. If there had been a fly there, it would have smashed it, the drop was so heavy.

'Hey,' I say. 'It's started! Rain!' I run my hands through my hair. 'That's good! See how much easier it is to breathe,' I say, inhaling. Ozone, fresh air! Power! 'Come on!' I shout, into the rain, as though all my problems are solved. Downpour, deluge, horizontal rain, torrent. I turn round, and shout delightedly: 'Hey, man, get this!' I stretch out my hand to encourage him to stand up.

But he goes on sitting as before. He waves my hand away.

'You don't know me either… You don't know anyone!'

He looks at me – viciously, damn it.

'What the hell's got into you, enjoy it, look…!'

'You're a fool!'

Well, fucking hell! Suddenly something gives in me too. I'm aware of it, but I can't stop myself:

'You're talking crap, what the fuck are you on about! You've been banging on sadistically for the last two hours, some shit about eyelids, you're slobbering like an idiot, you've developed a whole theory …'

'It's not a theory!'

'What's "not a theory"? First it stings, then it hurts. It's a process…'

'I know that!'

Borivoj Radaković

'You don't know a fucking thing!'

'I *know* it!' He roars! He looks at me crazily. He's shaking. Suddenly I go numb. My body knows. I know what he's going to say. He speaks:

'*I* cut a guy's eyelids off! Like this!' As he made the movement, I could feel myself stiffen. He's transformed. 'I took a prisoner of my own! I cut them off! To see what would happen!' Then, through his teeth: 'So don't you talk shit!'

I'm reeling. He gets up, like a zombie, knocks over the table, falls backwards against the wall, stops himself, awkwardly. He's grey. My back is sodden with rain. He pushes himself off the wall. He tries to hold himself up on the table, but the table gives way, he falls towards me. I grab him to stop him falling, but he grasps me. He disgusts me and I'm scared. He's saying something. I hear glass shattering.

'Mira will kill me if the windows break!' I grab the excuse. I push him away with all my strength. I rush into the other room: the windows are wide open, the rain is pounding on to the parquet floor. I struggle with the curtains, my spine is tingling with fear, I turn round to see whether he has followed me. I close the windows. Bloody, fucking hell! The floor is soaked. I run into the bathroom for a cloth, there isn't one, I grab a towel. I don't look towards the balcony; the most important thing for me is not to see him. The most important thing is to pretend that there's no tension, that I'm carrying out routine actions. And not to hear him. I run back into the room, throw the towel on to the floor and mop it with my foot – I'm afraid of bending down. Rain is beating against the window. It's suddenly stifling in the room. I can hear my heart thumping.

'Hey, you still alive?' I shout, as casually as I can, as I rush to the bathroom. I throw the towel into the bath, and use another to dry my hands. I go to the kitchen; from there I look on to the balcony, but... he's not there. A new wave of fear breaks over me: he's hiding! He's going to kill me, fuck it! I don't know when I farted, I can just smell it. He's confessed to what he did, now he's probably ready for anything. 'Hey, where are you?' I shout, but there's no answer. A chill runs down my spine. 'Pero!' I glance frantically around me. I'm burning.

Damn your eyes, are you lying in wait for me?

I quickly take a knife from the drawer. I'll defend myself, fuck you, this is my apartment, this is where I live with my wife and daughter, and you're not bloody going to... I'll cut your throat! Where are you?

I hide the knife along my arm, go to the toilet. I think, maybe he went in there while I was in the other room. I lean against the door: 'Pero! You having a pee?' I don't know whether he's going to rush the door or leap on me from behind. I shudder from top to toe. I look round, then knock. Then again. I hold the knife ready. I open the door – he's not there. I go into the bedroom, then my daughter's room, I peer round the door, back to the kitchen – he's nowhere.

He's gone, damn his bloody nerve. You chose me to tell about the man you killed, fuck it? I throw the knife down on the table. I don't give a flying fuck for you or your eyelids or the war or your nerves. Not in my house. The knife is lying with its blade upwards on the table. I quickly put it back in the drawer so as not to look at it. It's a good thing he's gone, anything could have happened. He could at least have let me know, bugger him, and not left me shitting myself with fear... My hands are shaking as I take my mobile from my pocket to call him, but then I say, out loud: 'But who gives a fuck, you idiot.' You come here to tell me... I put my phone back in my pocket. 'You have to dump your crap in my life?' I light a cigarette.

I'm shaking all over as I pick up the chair and table. It's exactly like when that Pole met me in the underpass. Afterwards I dreamed about him, and now I'll dream about this lunatic. His nose was running, but he said that he had come to defend us, and that we didn't know how to appreciate that. A mercenary, fuck it. That they had a graveyard where they buried them. What did I care! He held me by the arm and wouldn't let me go. Fuck off!

Now it's pouring steadily. Calmly. A summer downpour. I stretch my arms out in front of me, palms up, and raise them to the rain. Drops beat on me, exploding. I bend over so that they fall on my head.

As though I'd been struck by lightning, as though I was weight-less! Pero is lying in front of the apartment block! Crumpled. I can't see his head. Several people are standing round him, some are running out of the block opposite. I hear an ambulance siren. 'Don't touch him,' I shout. 'Wait for me!'

But this is my moment! I take a step back from the railing. I stand calmly, my arms by my sides, and close my eyes. I stand for a moment or two. Then I step out decisively. I climb onto the railing, straighten up, press down on my feet, spread my arms, breathe deeply, and one, two, three and – there – I soar! I hold my breath in my lungs until I feel secure. The rain bothers me a bit, I haven't flown for a long time. I make a circle at the same height. I enjoy the tension in my shoulders. I shout from up here: 'Now you see you should have come to school that day! Then you'd be able to fly!' I move a little away from the building, then come back. On the fifth floor, I pick some flowers at the Marković flat as I pass. The ambulance arrives and a man and woman in white slowly get out of it. They are struggling to open an umbrella. 'Hey, Pero, don't worry,' I shout. 'I'll speak at your funeral!'

The people in white have almost reached him, so I drop down more quickly. At the second floor, I slow down. I spread my hands, my fingers, it's a big effort, but I stop. Before they get to him, I throw him a flower.

I rush out of the main entrance, push some women aside, reach him before the ambulance people, stand over him and shout: 'Did you jump on purpose? Did you fall by accident?' My legs give way, I fall on to my knees in his blood diluted by the rain and ask the corpse in a whisper: 'Did I push you?'

Concrete story

Edo Popović

They're sitting on the second floor of a nine-storey apartment block. He's smoking, drinking coffee and reading yesterday's evening paper. She's just come back from the market and is cursing butchers who sell rotten meat. It's a stifling, late spring day, he's naked to the waist, droplets of sweat sparkle among the hairs on his chest. She takes off her peach-coloured top and pours coffee.

'In this heat,' he says, 'everything droops, everything becomes limp, trees, and buildings, and cars, and even your tits.'

'Really,' she says, 'and what about your dick, does it go limp?'

A young dove sits on the branch of a birch tree that almost touches the balcony railing, watching them. It blinks suspiciously at them, they're too close, but even so, it doesn't fly away, just blinks.

'Look at its beautiful eyes,' she says. 'Two black, sweet little dots.'

'Listen to this,' he says. 'On Wednesday night four newspaper kiosks in Zagreb were robbed. The thief stole forty-eight condoms and a camera film from the kiosk in Baštijanova St, doing around 380 kunas' worth of damage to the firm.'

'Why the film?' she asks.

'So as to have it to hand,' he says. 'You see, if he'd had a condom in his pocket, he wouldn't have had to rob the kiosk. As it was, he felt like a screw, but the woman wouldn't do it without a condom. Imagine, a simple screw drove him to robbery!'

Concrete story

'As though you're any better,' she says.

'Well now,' he says. 'I don't know what that kiosk in Baštijanova St is like, but if push came to shove, I'd rob a kiosk where they sold beer. I'd take several cigars, a can of cold lager…'

'You've always got beer on the brain,' she says.

'There you go,' he says, 'interrupting me again. That's a really bad habit you've got into, I mean not letting a person finish his train of thought. You burst in, carrying on where I left off, you say what you think I think, and then you get cross about it.'

'But all I said was that you're always thinking about beer,' she says in a conciliatory tone.

'I'd be thinking about you, of course I'd be thinking about you too. I'd buy you, that is steal you, some perfume, if there was any. Really, do those kiosks have perfume?'

'I don't need perfume, but I'd really like some body lotion.'

'Of course, I'd steal you the most expensive body lotion, and some suntan cream as well.'

'Thanks, but I don't need suntan cream,' she says bitterly.

'Oh, come on,' he says dejectedly, 'the sea's not the only place in the world where it's sunny, it's sunny at Bundek as well.'

They didn't mention the sea all afternoon. In the evening they went to sit on the balcony to look at old photographs of seaside holidays, where their faces and the faces of their friends smiled up at them.

'To hell with it,' she said, 'I'd really like to go to the sea this year.'

He said nothing and rolled a cigarette.

Damn the sea, he thought. A mass of salt water, big deal! I can sit in the shade sipping beer anywhere. And how in God's name could we get to the sea? There's no cash. A prize in some newspaper? Fuck it, if they only handed out twenty years in prison, or a package of unpaid bills, I'd certainly win. Cars, flats, holidays, music stations and all that crap, that's for others. It's all a set-up, he thought, furious now.

I'm not interested in the sea so that I can tell people about it, she thought. But I would like to tan my tits and bum a bit, that really suits me. And I'd like to have the smell of the sea in my nostrils, taste it in my mouth and throat, that slight bitterness and the scent of iodine. You don't get that at Bundek. Only mud and broken bottles.

They sat for a long time without speaking, each lost in their own thoughts. They listened to the wind rustling in the birch trees and imagined they were waves splashing on the pavement. Stars fell on to the streets; all that shone in the sky were the windows of skyscrapers.

The night the carpenter danced the pogo

Edo Popović

The winter when Ingemar Stenmark skied his way to his third successive World Cup, we sold Christmas cards in the flower market, Igor, Karlo and I. In those years wine was mulled on cookers in restaurants, there was still a water pump in front of the Zagreb cinema, and one went to midnight mass in Palmotićeva St with the same intentions as one went after mass to the OK Apple. At least, that applied to the three of us. God wasn't in the picture then, but there was no shortage of faith. Instead of God, we believed in Strummer, whose voice was more convincing and more destructive than God's. The things he screamed were psalms to our ears.

So, we borrowed the money for a stand, and we solved the problem of Christmas cards through a team effort. Igor was about to graduate from the School of Graphic Design, Karlo had been regularly taking the entrance exam for the Academy of Art, several years running, while I was slogging my way through my fifth semester of Yugoslav Languages and Literature at the Arts Faculty. I was, actually, indifferent, but the two of them genuinely despised standard Christmas cards ('Puuuuure shiiiiiiit' – I can still hear Karlo's nasal drawl), so they decided to do something about it. And they did. Karlo drew a dozen studies of the birth of Christ, Igor organised the printing at a printer's in Trešnjevka and I was in charge of the slogans. Our cards had to be ab-so-lu-te-ly different from the others, they had to be ab-so-lu-te-ly the best, ab-so-lu-te-ly desirable and fucking unsurpassed. That was imperative. Earnings were secondary; we wanted, above all, to give Christmas a new dimension, in keeping with the times.

'This is a real revolution, a sea change,' babbled Igor as we arranged the cards on the stand on the first day. 'Folk'll go wild, you'll see.'

I didn't share his optimism. I mean, the cards were OK, only they exuded roughly the same degree of holiness as the cover of the first Sex Pistols album. Mary's appearance and style of dress were a little reminiscent of Patti Smith, Joseph's of Iggy, while Jesus looked like Sid Vicious in proportions of 1:4. Deeply ingrained in my memory is one image in which, instead of being in a stable, the carpenter, his wife, Jesus, Caspar, Melchior, Balthazar, the ox and the donkey are standing on a stage; Caspar is on drums, Melchior on guitar, Balthazar on bass, Joseph (in a Pistols T-shirt, with a beer in his hand) is dancing the pogo in front of the microphone, Mary, with the child on her back, is a groupie who has just clambered on to the stage, and the donkey and ox are standing beside a loudspeaker grinning insanely. The text, not in the least original, reads: 'Well, fuck it, it's Christmas.'

Business wasn't that brisk. Partly because of the daring images, partly because of the loud music, which made people give our stand a wide berth. Communication with potential customers was reduced to a minimum. And when someone did happen to stop in front of our stand, things went roughly like this.

Customer: (moving his lips) ....!

Igor: (shrugging his shoulders, spreading his hands and pointing to his ears) 'I can't hear!'

Customer: (pointing to the cassette player and turning his fingers from right to left).

The night the carpenter danced the pogo

Igor: 'What? Turn it down? No way!' (shaking his head).

The customer goes away.

Igor: (turning to Karlo and me) 'What does the bum know about The Clash!'

Once, when Karlo had gone to get new batteries for the player, some guy nearly bought our cards, he spent a good five minutes examining them. Igor hopped nervously from one foot to the other, and then lost patience and said: 'Well, oaf, are you going to buy something?', whereupon the oaf changed his mind and went to the next stand.

By Christmas Eve, we'd sold about fifty cards.

'Five a day, roughly, that's not so bad,' said Igor when we had gone to the Pula restaurant towards evening, to analyse the situation over a glass of mulled wine.

'We screwed up,' said Karlo resignedly, 'we overestimated the taste of the masses, launched our idea before its time.'

'No,' said Igor, 'we're in tune with the times, it's just that this rabble is living in the past. The fucking distant past.'

'Same difference,' said Karlo, 'but nothing can alter the fact that we've made a big fat loss. We owe for the stand, we owe the printer, we've spent a huge amount on food and drink, and, on top of everything, we're frozen stiff.'

The next Christmas in the flower market passed without us. That year Karlo passed the entrance exam to the Academy, and then immediately lost interest in painting. At the end of September Igor and I saw him off on a train to London, from where he has still not returned. Igor finished graphics, and now he's smuggling computers. What about me? I write. And every year around Christmas I think, if only for a moment, about that year's Christmas. We didn't go to midnight mass in Palmotićeva, or to the Apple. We celebrated Christmas in the courtyard of Karlo's apartment building in Nazorova St. We lit a fire in the yard, sat on logs, listened to Silent Night, drank tea with rum and spent the whole night throwing the unsold Christmas cards on to the fire, one by one.

The ballad of Mott the Hoople

John Williams

Mac was getting into something of a routine. Late in the morning he'd walk into town, head round to Tomas's office where Tomas would go through the routine of saying the money hadn't come through yet, and Mac would make an increasingly weary pretence of getting angry and Tomas would finally spring loose enough cash for Mac to make it through another day, and he'd go and get something to eat down by the old market, then wander down towards the railway station and head into the underground shopping mall there. He'd meander over to Dragan's record stall and Dragan would be unfailingly pleased to see him and would play him all the new CDs, looking anxiously at Mac for his opinion like the world cared what Mac thought about The Hives or The Queens of the Stone Age and then they'd leave the stall in the hands of Judit who had the clothes stall next door and they'd head for the little corner bar and drink a couple of Ožujskos and then head back to the stall where Mac would look around and find something he remembered from back in the day and say all right if I borrow this for a day or two and Dragan would slap him on the back and say take whatever you want man it's an honour and then Mac would head back to the flat with the copy of *Aladdin Sane* or *Electric Warrior* or *Houses of the Holy* or whatever and sit and listen and drink a little brandy till Kat came back from work.

Today he was listening to Mott the Hoople. The album called just *Mott* with 'All the Way from Memphis' and 'Honaloochie Boogie' on it and the poem by Yeats on the back, the one with the line about the best lacking all conviction while the worst are filled with a passionate intensity, which seemed to apply pretty well to everything in modern life, from nu-metal to what little he could understand of politics in the former Yugoslavia, but right now Mac wasn't thinking about politics, 'cos mostly this record that he remembered as a good-time blast turns out to be like a concept album about the downs of the rock'n'roll life and Mac's been listening to 'The Ballad of Mott' over and over and now he's moved on to the last track on the album, a mandolin-led ballad called 'I Wish I Was Your Mother', which has to be one of the saddest songs he's ever heard in his life, and at first he's thinking about Kat, feeling like he was old enough to be her father all right, but then he hits the lines that go *I watch your warm glow paling/I see your sparkle fading* and he can't help but think about Jackie back home in London and how he's been treating her these last few years and what he's doing now shacked up in Zagreb with Kat. Stuck inside of Zagreb with the rock and roll blues again.

Mac shouldn't have been in Zagreb for more than a night. Last date of a two-week tour spanning Greece, Italy, Slovenia and Croatia – places where first-generation English punk bands were still viewed with mysterious reverence. Mysterious to Mac anyway, who found it harder and harder to fathom why anyone on earth would want to pay to listen to a bunch of forty-year-old blokes hammer their way through songs they'd written in about five minutes when they were eighteen. But pay they did and, in the absence of anything much happening with Mac's new music, it was the one way he knew of earning a living and now and then, as they careered through 'Suzy's down the Launderette', or 'Brick in the Face', he could still feel the faintest of aftershocks, the slightest echo of how much fun it had been at the time.

The ballad of Mott the Hoople

*

Mostly, though, it was a slog, and never more so than when you finished your tour with a date at the Rock City on the edge of Zagreb and the guy who's promoting the whole tour, Tomas, is meant to be there with your money except he's there with a bunch of excuses and no money. The other three lads have got their tickets home next morning, so they fuck off, threatening all hell if Mac doesn't get them their money, and Mac, who'd been counting on the money to pay for his own flight back, has no choice but to stay there and wait for Tomas to come up with the dosh.

And while he's waiting he gets together with Kat, who works the coat check at Rock City and has legs like you'd never see on any woman in Britain who wasn't a supermodel, but which seems to be par for the course in Croatia.

And so three weeks had gone by and Tomas's excuses were getting vaguer and vaguer and maybe Mac was playing a waiting game or maybe he wasn't in any hurry to go home.

Something so easy about this life, reminded him of being young, late seventies after he jacked in the job at Alcan driving the forklift, signed on and played in the band. You had money for tea and chips and beer, you had a gig once a week and a place to kip, what more did you want? What more was there on offer back then?

Not like now, when your life was full of endless choices. The little pointless ones, going round Tesco's with Jackie and the kids deciding what kind of pre-packaged salad you wanted. And the big difficult ones, another tour of the back of beyond on the punk revival circuit for guaranteed money, or take a punt on trying to get some gigs with a new band, a fuzzed-up alt.country kind of thing he'd been working on.

So yeah, he couldn't deny it really was a relief being here. A bit of a regression too, to be sure. He felt bad about Jackie, of course, stuck there in Gospel Oak with the kids, but – and there was another thing — fact was he knew she would be coping. Most capable person he'd ever met in his life, Jackie. She'd have the kids sorted for school, then she'd be off to work, cook the dinner in the evening, probably have a couple of mates round, all of it done like she enjoyed it, not like she was a martyr or anything. And, time to time, he couldn't help feeling like there was no need for him to be there. Well, be honest, kind of mood he'd been in the past year, she was probably happier with him out of the way.

He was putting that theory to the test now all right. He'd better ring her. Feeling guilty now, *I curse you just for caring*, he'd phone her, tell her what was going on. Well, not that exactly, but he'd tell her he'd be home soon, just a few more days till he got the money. He wouldn't phone now, though, not from the flat. Better to phone from a payphone somewhere, street noise in the background. Plus he didn't want her calling back getting Kat on the line. Could you do 1471 internationally? He didn't think so, but no point in risking it. Last thing he wanted to do was rub Jackie's nose in it. Sure, she might suspect something, but long as it wasn't in her face Jackie wasn't the type to go stirring up trouble. *I don't mean to upset you/but there's so much crime to get through.*

He'd phone her tonight on the way to the club. Who was on tonight anyway? He found a flyer on top of the TV. Emyr was playing, a warm-up show before the big summer festival in Split. Amazing the feller still had that much of a following when he was just a second-rate Nick Cave clone from Wales, far as Mac could see. Thing was, though, Mazz was playing guitar with him.

Mazz was Mac's spar from way, way back in the day, both of them nearly men from yesteryear. They'd even been in a band together for a while, early nineties, Pixies kind of thing, last blast at rock and roll heroism, both of them a bit too cynical and a bit too old for it, amazing how the kids could smell that, your desperation. But he'd kept on working, Mazz. It was easier for a guitar player really, just to fit in with someone else's thing. Emyr's thing, for instance, all you needed was cheekbones, a black wardrobe and a fancy reverb pedal.

But still the prospect of seeing a familiar face got Mac up and into action. He put his leather jacket on, found his fags, left a note for Kat and headed down the club, see if he could catch Mazz at the sound check.

An hour or so later they were sat down, round the corner from the club in a neighbourhood bar, doing the rock and roll thing, hanging around aimlessly waiting for someone to do something.

'How's it been?' asked Mac, once they were settled with their Ozujskos.

Mazz shrugged, looking skinnier and more rock-and-roll tubercular than ever, in contrast to Mac who was about twice the size he had been — from beanpole to bouncer in twenty years of beer and full English. 'Same old same old,' he said finally. 'Emyr's being a posey twat, bass player's pulling all the girls and the drummer's a drummer. Greece was good, though. He's big there.'

Mac nodded. 'Yeah,' he said, 'I heard that,' trying not to let jealousy get to him. Hard to avoid it in this business, though. Specially when the only thing people wanted from you was cartoon punk nostalgia, while a poser like Emyr was treated like Baudelaire on ice. Still, none of it was Mazz's fault.

Mazz must have seen something pass across his face, though, 'cos he laughed and said, 'Christ, man, you don't have to tell me it's bollocks. So what are you doing here anyway?'

Mac sighed and ran through the whole shabby saga. Mazz nodded like one who knew all too well what Mac was talking about, the crap tours, the non-paying promoters.

'You think he's going to pay up?'

Mac thought about it for a moment. 'I dunno,' he said eventually.

Mazz looked at him carefully. 'You got a ticket back?'

'No,' he said, 'that's the thing really.'

'Oh shit, man,' said Mazz, 'you could ride with us on the bus, except we're jammed up already and the insurance...'

'Sure,' said Mac, 'don't sweat it. Anyway, I want to get this thing sorted,' as he said the words wondering what thing he was talking about. He'd meant the money but what came into his mind was Kat here and Jackie back home. What he meant was himself; his head was what needed sorting.

Later on, a lot later on, they were at the after-show. Kat was excited to meet Emyr, happy that Mac knew these people, he could see that, happy that she hadn't been taken in by some impostor, some guy said he was big in England once. And now she was talking to Mazz over at the bar and Mac was in that unlooked-for zone where no matter how much he drank he couldn't get drunk, just more and more morose.

He walked over to Kat, put his arm round her, whispered in her ear that they should go soon, but she wriggled out from under his arm and carried on talking to Mazz like she hadn't heard. Shit.

He nodded to Mazz, who barely noticed him either, his eyes all over Kat, as well they might be, girl was gorgeous. Funny how fast that faded on you, though, like buying guitars or clothes when it came down to it, way you looked at women. One in the shop always looked better than the one you had at home. Yeah, and the one you had on the side here was better than the one you had in your real home. Christ, he wished Jackie was here now, ready to give him the look said you've had enough, Mac boy, time to be getting you home.

But she wasn't. There were just Croatian guys in polo-necks who'd talk to him about music and shame him for how little he cared, and Dalmatian girlfriends of Kat's with their long legs and dark eyes and no, no he wasn't going to go there, but he had to talk to someone, couldn't just stand there watching Mazz drool over Kat, and there was Emyr over there standing by himself, the Croatians backing off him, leaving him his own space.

The ballad of Mott the Hoople

Mac walked over, thinking the bastard acts like he doesn't know who I am, I'll deck him, but Emyr just looked at him and drawled, 'How you doing, big man,' and Mac said, God knows why, 'Lost, that's how I'm doing,' and Emyr just stared at him for a moment then said, 'Me and all man, me and all. So, you want to get more lost?' and Mac just nods and then they're in the manager's office doing some nice fat lines of coke and it works like it always does, you don't do it too often, and for a while Mac's back to himself telling stories, Emyr saying you used to be inside, yeah, and Mac telling prison stories and Emyr lapping it up, this mummy's-boy priest of the dark side, and then the buzz starts to fade a little and so it's back into the office with Emyr, and Mazz and Kat are there too and they're waiting their turn and Kat has her hand tracing Mazz's cheekbone and Mac sees just what it's been, him and her, and knows just like that that it's over, him and her, and, worse, that maybe it never really started, there was never a connection there, just a balance, a girl not hardly a woman trying to find herself and a man trying to lose himself. *I wish I'd been your father/played houses with your sisters/wrestled with all your brothers.*

He had to get out of there. He walked up the stairs, nodded to the girl on cloakroom duty and out into the night air. He followed the tram track towards town, walked past the cathedral then wound his way up the hill into the old town, finally stopping to rest by the top of the funicular.

He looked down on the city as the dawn came up. He picked out the landmarks he'd learned over the past weeks; the station in the distance, the central square, the block where Tomas had his office.

Unbidden, a plan came to mind. Mac walked back down the hill alongside the funicular. At the bottom he turned left, cut across the square, then turned right into Gajeva, kept on going till he came to an all too familiar block. He stopped outside number 11. The board outside listed the twenty or thirty businesses that had offices somewhere in the rabbit warren of a building. The outer door was locked. Mac considered hitting a selection of bells at random, see if someone would buzz him in. Decided against it — you were nothing but suspicious at 6.30 in the morning. Instead he walked round the side of the building, saw an alley that led round the back, followed it, saw a wall he could climb, jumped it. Now he was in the back yard of the office building. He saw steps down to the basement. A door with nothing more than a Yale lock on it. Mac dug out a defunct credit card from his wallet and was through it in seconds. Inside the basement he passed the tailor's and the sex shop and the travel agent's and came to the door to Tomas's office. One firm shove from Mac's fourteen stone and he was in there. Time to collect his money and go. He knew Tomas kept ready cash in a box in a locked drawer of his desk. Nothing big, not enough to pay what he owed Mac, but surely enough for a ticket home.

He forced the desk drawer open, stuck his hand in to grab the box. Except there was nothing there. In fact there was nothing anywhere in the desk. No papers, no nothing. Tomas had done a runner.

Mac walked back out of the building, through the front door this time, closing it behind him with exaggerated care, thinking it really was a mighty long way down rock and roll, but finally he'd found the bottom.

He walked aimlessly back up Gajeva. He couldn't face going back to Kat's place, finding her there with Mazz, a situation where you had no right to shout or fight; no claim, no ties, no nothing.

Outside the Hotel Europa there was a van pulling up. A bleary-eyed forty-five-year-old in a Jack Daniel's T-shirt and a cowboy hat was getting out of it and walking into reception. Mac caught his eye. He'd been around the night before, had to be the road manager. He nodded to Mac, recognising a fellow traveller, and Mac followed him into reception making small talk. Emyr and the drummer were already sat there, slumped on chairs in the lobby, both of them still in last night's clothes. Mac walked over to Emyr, had a quick what happened to you man conversation, while keeping one ear open as the road manager buzzed a couple of rooms. Soon enough the bass player came down. No sign of Mazz, though. Road manager cursed, Mac waited. Finally Emyr spoke. 'Fuck him, he can fly back.' And then he offered Mac a ride.

Mac took it. He'd call Jackie on the way. He'd make it up to her. You know how it is, girl, the road goes on for ever and the party never ends. Yeah, sure. Who was he kidding? Who really made anything up to anyone? Either they loved you enough to forgive you or they didn't. All in all, Mac thought, Jackie did. And sitting in the van letting Zagreb fade behind him, one more forgotten tour stop, that seemed like the saddest thing of all. *It's no use me pretending/ you give and I do the spending/Is there a happy ending?/I don't think so.*

Distance

Anna Davis

'The Croatian language,' writes Gareth Parfitt, MP, in his diary, 'is aggressive and harsh. The words are very long so they speak them quickly, spitting them out like machine-gun fire.' He sucks on the end of his pen, gazing around at the hotel room. It's like any three-star hotel room you'd find in any European city. The mini-bar, the trouser press, the TV, the plastic key-card which switches on heating and lighting. The hum of the air-con. His preconceptions about this hotel – about Zagreb – were entirely wrong. He'd expected a war-torn Eastern bloc feel. Lots of grey concrete. Ruined buildings, ruined faces – that brave, haunted look. Not a bit of it.

'It's odd to think how one's language sounds to a foreign ear,' he writes. 'I don't suppose the Croatians imagine they speak like machine guns. To me, the Welsh language is beautiful. But the English think it sounds like phlegm being cleared from the throat.'

Gareth Parfitt has always considered Welsh his mother tongue. He spoke Welsh at home as a child and had his own children educated at a Welsh-speaking school. But he writes in his diary in English.

There's a knock at the door. Probably that British Council girl, come to remind him that they're all meeting in the foyer in half an hour to go over to the ambassador's for dinner. What would they do

Distance

if he decided not to go? That random straggle of writers, storytellers, Welsh language teachers – how would they manage without him to lead their group, to make the right noises and use the right cutlery, to thank the ambassador on their behalf at dinner? To say something correct and noble about Wales and Croatia.

'Come in.' He can hear the fatigue in his voice.

It's that young novelist, Evan Arthur, inching in the door with an embarrassed look on his fine-boned face. Shuffling about and not knowing what to do with his hands. Long delicate fingers.

Something flips over in Parfitt's stomach.

'Sorry to disturb you,' says the novelist. 'You said something about a spare tie…'

'Oh yes. Of course.' Parfitt gets up and goes to the wardrobe. His hands are shaking.

The boy looks baffled, standing there with the tie in his hands. When he glances up at Parfitt, his eyes seem to plead. 'I… um…'

But of course. He doesn't know how to tie it. Just look at him, for Christ's sake, in his chinos and crumpled shirt. Probably the smartest clothes he owns. He's never worn a bow tie in his life.

'Let me help you.'

Arthur takes a few steps into the room and Parfitt moves around behind him – not because he can't tie the tie from the front, but because he wants to stand behind the young man – to reach around him, to gaze at the back of the neck, at the shoulders, his own face unobserved.

'So, you having a good time?' asks the novelist. And even from behind, Parfitt sees the neck blush – knows how red the face must look. This is how people are with him now. They ask him an innocent question and then straight away they think they've invited a confession or hinted at something unseemly.

At the airport, this morning, he'd had a surprise. As he came shuffling through the barrier with the rest of the 'Wales–Croatia Cultural Festival' rabble, heaving their rucksacks, dragging their little cases on wheels, he'd been confronted by the familiar flash of cameras, the microphones jabbing like spears, the eager, hungry faces with notebooks at the ready, and he'd just had time to mutter 'Here we go again' when he realised that it was Evan Arthur they were after. They were swarming after the novelist, while the ex-minister of education sidled through to the waiting British Council minibus totally unnoticed.

'I'm having a fine old time.' Parfitt allows his hands to brush against Arthur's neck. The skin is soft and warm. 'How about you?'

'Incredible!' says Arthur. His hair is a wonderful golden colour. And downy, like a child's. 'In England nobody gives a shit about writers. I felt like a pop star this morning. D'you know how it feels to be the centre of attention like that? To have all those journalists and TV people wanting to talk to *you*?'

'Oh yes.' And Parfitt sees that the neck is red again as the novelist realises his blunder. 'It's a bit different for me, though.'

The food at the ambassador's is bad. The meat is under-seasoned, the vegetables overcooked. The new potatoes have the texture of cotton wool. It's always like this when you dine with British diplomacy abroad. As if the local cooks deliberately dumb down in the belief that Brits Eat Bland. Not like the lunch Parfitt treated himself to when he went wandering through the town earlier on. No menu to order from – the waiter just brought out plate after plate of the most delicate, peculiar shellfish, washed down with the lightest golden wine and some shots of a strong colourless spirit. Eating alone is such a poignant joy.

He's sitting now between the ambassador's horsey wife and a slightly overweight thirty-something female novelist with garish shoes on bare feet and a face speckled with eczema. The novelist, who has clearly never been away on a trip of this kind before, is pelting the Croatian university lecturer opposite with a barrage of questions.

'How was it during the war? Were many people killed in Zagreb?'

'The war never came to Zagreb,' says the lecturer. 'Though you could hear the bombs falling in the distance.'

The novelist, momentarily disappointed, is visibly delighted with the second half of the lecturer's pronouncement. Parfitt can just see her trying to imagine it, romanticising the sound of falling bombs.

'It is very strange,' says the lecturer, 'that you are not wearing any socks. Aren't your feet cold?'

'No,' says the woman novelist. 'Not at all.'

'In London they wear whatever they like, whether it's hot or cold,' says an intense Croatian with grizzled grey hair. 'In London, nobody stares.' He has actually been staring at Parfitt all evening. All bloody day, in fact. He's been hanging around with the Welsh group ever since they walked into the airport, though Parfitt has no idea who he is. He's certainly not with the British Council, that's for sure. There's something demonic about him – those black eyes, that jagged brow.

Garish Shoes is not interested in talking about London or her feet. She's asking the lecturer more questions about life in Zagreb.

'It's very expensive,' says the lecturer. 'People struggle to survive.'

And yet when Parfitt went out walking today, everybody seemed to be tall, young, beautiful, and rich-looking – with designer clothes and mobile phones. Only at the marketplace did he see the headscarfed women in bad knitwear that he'd expected. They came from outside the town, of course, these women. They were selling vegetables.

The ambassador's wife asks Parfitt something inconsequential – something he doesn't even hear. He realises she's not spoken throughout the meal – an utterly bizarre phenomenon from a woman of this sort – the hostess, indeed! But of course it's him that's the problem. She has been struggling for something safe to say. And now that she's found it, he hasn't even heard her. A timely moment, perhaps, for him to speak up to the assembled group, to thank His Excellency on behalf of the Welsh visitors ...

By the time the evening is over, Parfitt is drunk. Not that it shows — he's good at being secretly drunk. Ripping the bow tie from his neck as they all come stumbling out of the ambassador's residence into the fresh night air, he finds Evan Arthur talking to the grizzled grey Croatian, and asks, 'So, where are we going now?'

It's obvious, when they get to the jazz club, that nobody had expected him to go with them. He's not one of them. Worse, he's a politician (although hardly that any more). That's why the grey-haired man looks at him in that demonic way. The grey-haired man is an anarchist, so Garish Shoes tells Parfitt at the bar. He doesn't respect people who have aligned themselves with the Establishment.

Parfitt finds himself buying beers for the whole group. There's the two novelists, the grey-haired Croatian and a whole extra bunch of Croatians who were already here when they arrived. The rest of the Welsh group have gone back to the hotel. The two novelists, he realises, as he ferries beer over to the long table and returns to the bar to collect more, are not here because they're enthusiastic about Welsh politics or arts or the Welsh language. They both have books coming out in translation and they want to promote them and party. The Welsh thing is a side issue — a way of getting their expenses paid. The grey-haired man is their true host, and these are their people ...

But who are *my* people?

The jazz band is packing up. Everybody is smoking and drinking fast. Parfitt buys more beers and yet more. It's clearly his job to do so. There's all this machine-gun-speak at one end of the table and a woman is laughing on and on. She has huge teeth and a shrill voice. He wishes she'd shut up. He'd like to slap her. He's

Distance

stuck beside Garish Shoes, who is determined to talk to him about Welsh things. Well, at least she's found something to say to him.

'I was at your talk this afternoon,' she says. 'I thought it was very good.'

'Thank you.' At the other end of the table, seemingly in deep conversation with the grey-haired man, is Evan Arthur, a cigarette dangling between gentle fingers. He's not just attractive, Parfitt realises. He's beautiful. He has a perfect rosebud mouth.

'Funny that it was so well attended, though, don't you think?' says Garish Shoes. 'I mean, why should Croatians be interested in Welsh devolution?'

'I haven't the first clue,' says Parfitt, still staring at Arthur. Wondering: straight or gay? Maybe Garish Shoes would know. If he could only find a way of asking.

'Evan and I did a radio reading this afternoon in front of an audience,' says Garish Shoes. 'And do you know what I got asked? "Are you planning to write your next book in Welsh?" Can you *imagine*? I told them I don't speak Welsh and the guy who asked the question looked at me like I was a traitor. It's the nationalist thing, you see. They identify with the Welsh. They think we're the same at some deep level.'

'Well, aren't we?' Parfitt is only half listening.

Garish Shoes comes over all annoyed. 'Don't be ridiculous. In what way does our experience resemble theirs? This whole festival is ridiculous. You, giving your talk on devolution. Those bloody teachers running Welsh language classes. I mean, what the hell use is the Welsh language to someone from Zagreb?'

'The classes are fully subscribed,' says Parfitt. Down the table, Evan Arthur has turned to talk to the laughing girl, and now she reaches out and pinches his cheek playfully. Parfitt feels as if someone just stabbed him.

'You don't get it, do you?' says Garish Shoes.

'I'm sorry?'

Evan Arthur has brown eyes like that boy. The boy in the park. He saw the eyes, that night, by the glow of the cigarette lighter.

Garish Shoes is getting in a temper. 'This is an amazing place,' she snaps. 'It's my second time here. I couldn't wait to come back. It's like Paris in the 1920s. The writing scene is young and exciting. I've read my work in a nightclub at one o'clock in the morning, in English, to an audience of over three hundred people. Do you think it's like that in London? Do you think it's *ever* been like that?'

'I don't see what this has to do with the Welsh classes.' Parfitt is dizzy and dry mouthed. He needs more beer, but if he gets up he'll end up buying beer for the whole table yet again. Evan looks like the boy he followed that night in the park.

'It could be so good here,' says Garish Shoes. 'It *is* so good. But then some cunt in a radio reading audience starts in on you because you don't speak Welsh when it's supposed to be your mother tongue, and then you remember what happened here a few years ago – the rampant nationalism. The feelings and beliefs that start wars. And here comes a bunch of idiots from Cardiff with their stupid Welsh language lessons. And here comes Gareth Parfitt with his talk on Welsh devolution. Bet you never gave a second thought to who your audience would be. Bet you just trot out the same talk every time. Don't suppose you have much else to do these days, do you?'

'Excuse me,' says Parfitt, getting to his feet. 'I'm going to the bar.'

At the bar, trying to breathe, he orders another round of beers. All he can see are those eyes in the park, lit for just an instant by the cigarette lighter. Coaxing him on. The boy asked him for a light and started to walk away, leaving Parfitt to follow ... And when he gets back to the table, he is relieved to see that Garish Shoes has moved over to talk to Grizzled Grey-hair. The beers are seized the moment he sets them down, so that he has to go back and order an extra one for himself. Garish Shoes' seat has been taken by the

Croatian university lecturer who was at the ambassador's dinner. He's only just arrived, and seems in search of someone to talk to. Latches on to Parfitt.

The room is slipping and sliding now. The heavy red walls are closing in. Parfitt can hardly breathe for the smoke. The lecturer is blathering in his ear but Parfitt has no idea what he's saying. The grizzled grey man stares at him with demonic eyes. He feels sick. Look at them all, this bunch of writers and hangers-on – so smug, so sure of themselves and their dull little alternative scene. They think they're so fucking interesting, don't they. He'd like to grab them all by the throat and shout, What the hell do you know? Cooped up in your studious little rooms with your computers and your egos. Some of us have had to make decisions that could change millions of lives. Millions! Some of us have more important things to think about when we get up in the morning than what to have for breakfast!

And then it's all over and you end up buying the beers.

Evan Arthur is beautiful enough to break my heart.

'Hey, where are you going?' asks the lecturer.

'I'm off,' says Parfitt. 'I've been to livelier funerals than this.'

The mini-bar is dry. Tiny bottles litter the anonymous hotel floor. Through a thick boozy fug, Parfitt hears them outside his door. Two voices – a woman and a man.

'That lecturer kept going on about the fact that I'm not wearing any socks.'

'Maybe he wanted to sleep with you.' That's Evan. Evan and Garish Shoes.

'Nah. Oh, did you hear what Parfitt said when he left?'

'What?'

'*I've been to livelier funerals than this.* That's what he said.'

'Where do you reckon he went?'

'Well, that's the golden question, isn't it. Where does someone like that go to have a livelier time?' Her awful mocking voice.

'I feel a bit sorry for him.'

Parfitt groans and rubs his pulsing head. He's slumped on the floor, still dressed, and the lights are still on. The hum of the air-con. There's a line of dry spit down one side of his face.

'I've got a mate who used to work for him,' says Garish Shoes. And there's an odd muffled sound. Is she actually leaning against the door of his room while they're out there talking about him? Doesn't Evan remember that this is his room?

'She was one of his researchers when they were still in opposi-tion,' she continues. 'She told me none of them knew. If anything, she had him down as a bit of a ladies' man.'

'I suppose he kept it pretty secret,' says Evan.

'She said he was always awkward, though. You know, socially. She said it was really hard trying to make conversation with him in the lift of a morning. She'd sooner take the stairs. That's weird, don't you think? For a politician to be so awkward?'

'Oh, I don't know,' says Evan. 'They're human, like the rest of us. I guess he had problems.'

'I guess. Well … goodnight, then.'

' 'Night.'

He hears the high-pitched beep as a key-card is pushed into its slot. Sounded like it came from the room next door.

Who was this 'mate' of Garish Shoes who used to work for him? Karen? Louisa? More likely Siobhan – she was the real gossip … Oh hell, what did it matter anyway.

Which one of them has the room next door? Evan or Garish Shoes?

Parfitt goes to the bathroom and drinks water out of the tap. Lots and lots of it. Then pisses, barely able to stand up straight, getting some on the seat.

He's about to switch out the light and go to bed when he changes his mind, fetches out his diary and pen.

Distance

'Here's the thing,' he writes. 'The most I have ever done is light a man's cigarette in a park and follow him and get mugged by his friends. Nobody would ever believe this – not the Prime Minister, not my wife, not my constituents. But it's true. I have never had sex with a man. The most I have done is think about it and dream about it and want it. My biggest crime is to draw attention to myself – something I seem to be very good at. I resign, even though there is nothing to resign over. I say provocative things to random people in bars. I make so-called serious speeches about Welsh devolution to random groups of people in faraway countries. Nobody wants to hear me talk on Welsh devolution in Wales.

'I do all this because I am trapped. I am trapped.'

He rips the sheet of paper from his diary – the diary he's been keeping these last few months in the hope that he might produce a book that someone might want to publish. Trouble is, he has no story.

He opens his door and totters out into the corridor in his bare feet. With difficulty, he bends, almost overbalancing, and stuffs the piece of paper under the door of the next room.

And then he is tired, and he sits down on the floor and closes his eyes.

Yogurt for Nina

Zorica Radaković

She was tempted to pour herself a glass of 'heart medicine', but she resisted. And, while the Persian cat looked at her from the sink, where it was watching the dripping tap, Blaženka sat wearily at the table, smoking and adding up on her calculator all the outgoings she had loaded on to her credit cards.

'Is there anything to eat, Mum?' Nina appeared at the kitchen door.

'Sure.' She put out one of the two cigarettes that were burning in the ashtray. 'I bought bread, and there's yogurt in the fridge.'

'There isn't any yogurt, Mum!'

'Yes there is, I told him not to touch it.'

'Do you want to check?' Nina opened the fridge door.

All there was in the fridge was margarine, a tin of cat food and a carton of iced tea.

'Oh, damn his eyes…' She hissed bitterly and put her hand to her heart.

'Please don't talk about Dad like that!'

'I mean…' Nina tossed back the bush of her long curly fair hair and crossed her arms over her chest. 'You sort things out between you as best you can, but don't shout at each other in front of me. I really don't know why I should always be the one to be victimised!'

'You victimised?' Blaženka raised her spectacles. 'How, may I ask, are you victimised?' The blood had rushed to her head and she felt like blurting out the whole burden of truth, which she had not wished to trouble Nina with up to now. But Nina had already begun to complain.

'Easily! I don't drink, or smoke, I don't even drink fruit juice! I drink water! Only water, get it! I don't even eat meat, Mum ...'

'And that's why you're so pale and tense!'

'What I mean is ...' She raised her voice. 'I spend less than anyone in the whole of Zagreb! I don't ask for anything. I'm either at uni or I'm studying for exams. When things are quiet, I mean, and I don't have to go to Sandra's to study with her. And then ... and then there isn't even a yogurt for me!'

'That's your father's fault!' At that exclamation, the cat leapt off the sink and appeared immediately at Nina's feet. 'Just accept that and grow up! If it weren't for me ...'

Nina picked up the cat, pressed it to her, then turned and went out, offended.

Blaženka's face twitched. Resisting the urge to run after her daughter and have the whole thing out with her, she lit a new cigarette with a trembling hand. Her belly and chest heaved, while her heart beat increasingly fast.

She went to the little cupboard where she kept herbs and supplies of drink. She opened the door shakily, and when she reached for the bottle of brandy the page of an old calendar stuck to the inside of the door caught her eye.

The picture showed Nina aged seven. In a dinner jacket, her hair combed like a boy's, she was sitting at a concert piano, a violin in her hand. Her daddy, Damir, a film producer then, was proud of his little girl's beauty, so he had pulled strings so that the child could be a model. That was how her sweet face came to be beaming from advertisements for the most prestigious producer of confectionery in the whole of what was then Yugoslavia.

She drained the glass in two or three rapid gulps, then filled it again. She was too agitated to count and for a few moments she simply stared blankly at the pile of hateful bills and lottery tickets. Then she suddenly swore and swept them all violently off the table.

'Bugger life if you can't dress decently for a wedding!'

She had been racking her brains for days now, trying to think up ways of generating money to buy party clothes for herself, Damir and especially Nina. She could not have borne to have people feeling sorry for her or laughing at her on that occasion.

In her nightmare imagination she saw her distant relatives talking: 'Who's that good-looking girl in rags?' 'Oh, that's poor Blaženka's daughter: the poor woman does nothing but slave for the girl and her husband!' And then she could imagine her malicious sister-in-law adding: 'She's spent so long manoeuvring with bankers' cards and cheques, loans and credit, that she could become a stockbroker!' Then she saw a third person asking who they were talking about and them saying: 'Oh, no one!'

And she had once been someone, a real expert! An engineer of wood technology! She had been on the point of becoming director of production when that particular state enterprise fell apart. She was forty then, a dismissal note in her hand, an unemployed husband and a daughter at school! She did not lose heart, but accepted a job as an ordinary salesperson at the counter in a firm dealing in wood. She thought it would be temporary, that is why she never told Nina what it was like to spend eight to ten hours a day in wood shavings and sawdust, stifling in summer and freezing in winter. She consoled herself that there was an economic crisis and without a murmur she spent regular and overtime hours receiving orders, and then measuring and cutting large planks of veneer and chipboard. And she kept smiling! She smiled and asked her customers to repeat several times exactly what they wanted so that her boss would not deduct the price of wrongly cut pieces from her pay. And he did that – to the last penny!

Yogurt for Nina

Nina did not know that her mother had never complained to her boss, a capitalist parvenu, that she feigned dedication, she was even meek with the man who stole from her by cheating the law and saving on tax, paying her the minimum salary, which meant that in her ever closer old age she would have an insignificant pension. While Nina, without a care in the world, studied for high marks so that she would be able to carry on with postgraduate studies, she did not know how much her mother hated herself while she listened to her boss's laments about the hard times, about his expenses, about himself, poor man, who was obliged to set aside part of his working profit for bribing the financial inspectors. And how she disgusted herself when she asked him for an advance, which he generously gave her in the manner of a benefactor, full of bogus concern for 'his' people. And while he tapped her on the shoulder in fake warmth, they both knew that he would slap huge interest on the loan. Nor did Nina know what it was like to be afraid to ask for a day off to go to the doctor because your heart was battering your rib cage every night, for this whole daily performance of humiliation was no guarantee that you would not be dismissed. Nina did not know what fear was. While her father loafed around in pubs, complaining that incompetent politicians meant that decent people like him had no jobs, and playing poker machines, Nina studied. And so she should.

The brandy acted on her bloodstream, and the tension in her chest eased.

Good, at least the wedding present was there – a large Venetian glass vase, which she had bought on her neighbour's credit card. That was a consumer coup! A large shopping centre on the edge of town had offered a huge discount and two-year repayment terms to customers who spent thousands of kunas there. Her neighbour was buying a television and he needed several more buyers, in order to arrive at the desired sum through a combined effort. Blaženka was delighted at the opportunity. It was heaven-sent. She decided to fulfil the conditions for the discount herself. So she bought a new well-known brand of vacuum cleaner, a washing machine, an answerphone, a music station and the large expensive vase that had caught her eye. She worked out that, at 450 kunas a month, she would probably manage, even if she didn't win the lottery.

But problems with payments began with the very first instalment. She barely succeeded in placating her neighbour into waiting a day or two until her mother's pension and social supplement had been paid into her bank. Her mother grumbled, admittedly, but she did bale her out with half her pension. She'd need money for the coming month as well, so she had to persuade her mother that it would be a real sin not to take a loan from a local bank which, as part of the government's social policy, offered pensioners immediate credit, with no surety and modest annual interest.

As the months went by, more and more people became involved in her finances, but Blaženka, as she relaxed over a drink after a hard working day, knew how to justify herself because she was not borrowing for luxuries, just for survival. The only thing was, after many glasses, one after another, she did not dare think about the future, which, if she did not win the lottery, was looking like a dark tunnel. Because the legacy, which her husband had received after his parents' death, had all been spent on old gambling debts, a Versace suit and several pairs of shoes, and what she as one of three beneficiaries could expect after her mother's death would have an insignificant impact on her fundamental financial recovery.

Blaženka worked and borrowed, and borrowed in order to pay back, and she believed that one day better days would come, at least for Nina. At the same time, Nina was becoming increasingly estranged from her, and changing. It had been a long time since she had resembled the little girl on the calendar.

Blaženka poured another glass of courage. She knocked on Nina's door.

'What do you want? Why are you bothering me?' She heard

Yogurt for Nina

Nina's voice from inside. 'I'm studying…'

She opened the door and, concealing her fuddled state, slowly entered the room.

Nina was sitting at her desk, bent over typescripts, and beside the desk, on the bed, lay Lina, gazing inquisitively at Blaženka with her large amber eyes.

'I don't like you standing behind me,' said Nina, not turning towards her mother.

Blaženka moved a step or two away, then sat down on the bed beside the cat.

'There, now I'm not behind you…'

Nina half turned to her and snapped at her irritably:

'Look, Mum, not now…' and went back to her reading.

Blaženka looked at her daughter's profile. She was now a grown-up young woman who no longer seemed to need her support. Her bearing exuded self-confidence, even the threat that, as soon as she came by some income, she would plunge into an independent life in which there would no longer be any space for her. Blaženka trembled at the terrible thought.

'You're not being fair… You're put out because of one little yogurt… While I'm wondering how to come by the money for a dress and shoes for you…'

Nina sighed deeply, looked at the ceiling, and drummed her nails on the desk.

'But, Mum…! Isn't it enough that I'm going to that circus at all, and now you want to dress me up! You haven't got the money for a piddling yogurt, and you're dreaming of evening dress!'

'Nina, darling, don't you worry about anything. I'll make the money, and you'll have a dress. I've already looked in the boutiques. There are such elegant dresses, nicely cut, just for your figure… Come and take a look… When are you going to show yourself off, if not now?' She sighed. 'Nina, darling, I'll steal from the till, if necessary! The skinflint has made a mint out of us…'

'Calm down, Mum!' Nina banged her hand down on her papers.

'What do you mean, "calm down"? Do you think I'm drunk?' She waved her hand and knocked over the glass full of pens that stood on the desk.

'Yes, you're drunk, and that's why I'm asking you to stop it. That's enough! Please, go and sleep,' she said, gathering the pens and putting them back in the glass. 'Don't let Dad see you like this.'

'What about your dad? What about him? Tell him he's drunk! Tell him he's a gambler. The idiot. There's no one he hasn't borrowed from, the wretch! He ate your yogurt! The waster!'

'Stop it, Mum!'

'Why should I? Grow up once and for all, take a look at what's happening to you! I work my fingers to the bone, I lick my boss's arse, I ...' She covered her face with her hands. 'And you won't even dress decently for a wedding for me.'

'It's enough that I'm going to the wedding!'

'And when you get married, then it'll be a different story!'

'Me! Never! Not on your life!' Nina shook her head in disgust.

'Never what, on my life?'

'I'm never getting married!' Flushed, she brought her face right up to her mother's and looked into her red, drunken eyes.

Blaženka gave a start in alarm and asked barely audibly why not.

'What if I told you that boys don't attract me at all?'

'What do you mean by that?' Blaženka felt the alcohol suddenly drain from her.

'What you heard.' She looked into her eyes.

'It's not true, Nina!' She stood up abruptly like a scalded cat.

'Think what you like. But I've no intention of ending up like you.'

'I see!' She shot her a withering glance. 'Women are more important to you than your mother?'

*

Yogurt for Nina

When Damir came home, several hours later, carrying a bag with three portions of meatballs in pitta bread, went into the kitchen and saw the empty brandy bottle and heap of papers on the floor, he hurried to the bedroom, with Lina wrapping herself round his legs. Blaženka was lying in her clothes, half covered, her face the colour of ash. There was a strong smell of alcohol and stomach acid in the air.

'Hey, old girl!' He shook her. 'Blaža! Blaženka…'

'Aaaah…' she replied, without opening her eyes.

'Come on, wake up…' He leaned over her face and rubbed her nose with his. 'Blaža, come on…'

'Huh?' Blaženka shivered at his touch.

Glad that she had woken without serious problems and without the stiffness that sometimes locked one side of her body, he smiled cheerfully.

'Hi, old girl…' he said in the tone of a playful child who would do anything not to be punished for a prank. 'You OK?'

'What happened to that yogurt, eh?' she asked in a hoarse voice.

'Bugger the yogurt! Come on, get up, I've brought meatballs. Come on! And call Nina while I wash my hands…'

'What kind of meatballs?' Blaženka still hadn't opened her eyes.

'Normal meatballs. With onion. For lunch.'

'Lunch at this time of day?'

'All right, supper! Come on, let's go before they get cold!' He rubbed his hands.

Blaženka suddenly raised herself on to her side, propping herself on her elbow.

'Have you been gambling? Damn you…'

'No, I haven't. Didn't I tell you yesterday that's all behind me? Gambling for me is…'

'Who did you borrow from?' Blaženka sat up on the edge of the bed. 'Are you crazy? Are you… Isn't it enough that the mafiosi come to your door to get it back?'

'I earned it!'

'You earned it?'

'On a bet!' And not waiting for Blaženka's next attack, he went on, his face glowing. 'It was Pero, you know Pero, the butcher. Well, he said that Yugoslavia beat Zaire at the World Cup in Germany nine-one. But I said it was nine-nil, OK, then, phone 9400.' He bent closer to Blaženka: 'Sports Information!' Then he showed his middle finger. 'I had him, didn't I? And so, here are the meatballs! Come on, call Nina, let's go and eat before they get cold.' He set off towards the kitchen, but went on, louder, for Blaženka to hear. 'Who does he think he is! I'm an encyclopedia of football for him. And I'm an idiot, we ought to have bet a suckling pig!'

He put plates on the table, and then opened the little cupboard to take out a bottle of beer. His eye fell on the calendar:

'My sweetheart!' He blew her a kiss, and then turned towards the kitchen door. 'An encyclopaedia of sport! That's what I am!' He turned back to the cupboard. 'Blaža, isn't there anything else to drink?'

The cat was winding herself round his legs, and he went over to the table, took one meatball from his plate, crumbled it, removed the onion and, blowing on it to cool it, bent down and held out his hand:

'I haven't forgotten you, of course I haven't forgotten my beauty ...'

Blaženka was standing leaning in the doorway:

'That onion stinks ... and the grease ...'

She went up to the laid table and lowered herself on to a chair with difficulty. Damir came up to her, hugged her and asked innocently:

'Have you had a little ...? A bit of brandy?'

'Get away ...' said Blaženka, pushing him away from her.

'Where's Nina?' he asked as he washed his hands.

'How should I know?' said Blaženka, scowling, and picking up a meatball in her fingers. 'Why did you get three portions?'

'There are three of us, aren't there?'

'But you know Nina's vegetarian.'

'Oh, fuck it…' Damir was quite downcast. 'I forgot. I ought to have bet a vegetarian pizza.'

Blaženka was still holding the meatball in her fingers.

'What's up, why aren't you eating?'

Blaženka just looked straight in front of her.

'Well?'

Blaženka didn't raise her eyes, but murmured hoarsely:

'Our Nina's a lesbian.'

'Who with?'

'It doesn't matter who with, you fool, but that's what she is! Our daughter's a lesbian! Do you know what that means?'

Over the next few days Blaženka pretended in her daughter's presence that she didn't remember her confession, but with Damir she was open. Damir tried in vain to take her mind off pessimistic images, in which, if Nina's lesbian leanings became known, they would lose credibility as a family and the respect of all their relatives, and the same with their friends and acquaintances, and Nina would experience great problems and obstacles at work and in social contacts, in life altogether. Damir did what he could to take Blaženka's mind off the idea that their daughter had a disturbed emotional side to her personality and urged her to think about herself and her body instead, to go to a doctor and have her heart seen to, to find out once and for all whether it was a matter of hypoglycaemia or a heart defect or just acute cardiac tension. But she wasn't interested in any issue that deflected her from thoughts of her daughter's homosexual orientation.

She thought about it as she moved around the sawmill with a smile on her face, carrying cut pieces of chipboard, while she brushed Lina's fur, while she bought supplies on credit in their little local supermarket, while she cooked, drank a glass of brandy and watched television. And when she fell asleep, she would be roused from the deepest dream with a sense of horror, and she would wake Damir and ask him to have a word with Nina and find out whether by any chance she was just joking.

'But I can't ask the child out of the blue: "Listen, darling, is it true that you're really a lesbian?" ' he protested.

Then he would get up, go to the kitchen and smoke, feed Lina and play with her, then make himself a coffee.

One morning, when they were having breakfast together, and when Nina was in such a good mood, because of an exam she had passed the previous day, that a touch of colour had returned to her face, otherwise white and soft as Botticelli's Venus, Damir asked:

'I don't want to meddle in your affairs, but Mum says... I mean, I'm asking because of her... Is it true that you... aren't interested, that's to say, how shall I put it... in boys?'

'Yes, Dad, it's true.' She raised her head. 'Should I explain that it's not a disease and defend myself? Do you want me to feel guilty?'

'No, my beauty! You're not guilty of anything...'

She looked at him and smiled.

'Thanks, Dad. I wasn't completely sure, but I believed you would understand.'

'OK, OK. Of course, I'm not exactly delighted, but...' He shrugged his shoulders. 'Only, make things easier for Mum, please. Tell her it's not true.'

'You want me to lie to her?'

'For her sake, please.' Damir put his head on one side, pleadingly. 'At least for a time.'

'I'll see,' replied Nina, sighing painfully.

The days passed, but Nina did not retract the news her mother found so hard to take. And then her cousin Anica's wedding day arrived.

Yogurt for Nina

Blaženka put on a cashmere dress from an exclusive boutique which an old school friend had lent her, Damir put on his Versace suit, and Nina an elegant pink dress and shoes. They took the Venetian glass vase, hailed a taxi and, as though they hadn't a care in the world, cheerful and proud, set off for the ceremony.

Among all the other relatives, acquaintances and unknown people, with their glittering jewellery and fragrant perfumes, they went into the town hall, smiling, like a happy family from an advertisement.

'Isn't she beautiful?' Blaženka asked her husband in a whisper as they went into the registrar's room.

'The bride is wonderful.'

'I don't mean the bride! Our Nina! She's the most elegant and the most feminine girl here.'

When the buzz of talk died down, the registrar and his assistant greeted the bride and groom and the assembled company, and then, in the same solemn tone, began to read the law on marital relations. And then came the moment when the couple pronounced their 'I do's', the moment when there was not enough oxygen, and the young couple's mothers suppressed tears of joy, then the exchange of rings, signing the register, photographs.

Blaženka was happy for her niece, but her heart couldn't take it.

'Why didn't you tell her, in God's name!' Damir had banged his fist on the kitchen table, which made Lina, who was sitting by the sink watching the water dripping from the tap, leap to the floor and flee.

The family dispersed. Nina waited until she was certain that no one could hear her. And then that moment came. She bent down and took a handful of soil.

'I'm not a lesbian, Mum,' she whispered, and threw the soil into the grave.

The last stretch of the way

Gordan Nuhanović

'We must make the most of these nice days.' Karmen sighed, lifting her face to the increasingly distant warmth of the sun. The lamps were flickering; it was the end of the working day and people they passed as they walked seemed out of breath, as though they were breathing through their mouths because a south wind was blowing steadily, aimed very precisely at their faces.

At that time Sabina was increasingly prone to waves of regret. Like many people she knew, like many with whom she later exchanged experiences, Sabina too had reached, surprisingly quickly, in her early thirties, a point where she simply did not want to hear anything about her relatives in the provinces. The period of late socialism had dictated a style of life generated by industrialisation and large-scale migration, which had shaped her. Families had become stratified and people, preoccupied with their jobs and commitments, shrank quite openly from emotional exploitation. Those were the years of Sabina's prosperity; she had a husband, two sons and a very responsible job in a firm, that, a few years later, would emerge from privatisation graced with foreign capital. That was all enough for her to believe that she was on the right track, but since this distant cousin had appeared Sabina seemed to want to make up for everything she had missed out on over the years. She asked about everyone in turn, where they were, what they were doing, and Karmen gave her very full information about illnesses, affairs and the professional circumstances of the entire family. Sabina had evidently missed a multitude of deaths, but also the occasional birth, and in the meantime her village had acquired asphalt and a community hall and for some reason that pleased her.

The two of them had their favourite café at that time – actually it was a restaurant, built of simple brick, a kind of university annexe, where students like Karmen, from outside town, used to go. The music played there was full of secret hints of rebellion and the promise of eternal love, unlike the conversations, which were accompanied by yawns with tears of boredom in the eyes.

'Did you have a dreadful day at work?' Karmen asked. Sabina chewed her lower lip and trembled barely perceptibly; to an extent she was alarmed by such perceptiveness on her cousin's part, and it seemed to her that it was stupid to hide such obvious things as dejection and bad humour. Then she took a business card out of a pocket in her wallet and put it down in front of Karmen like a card player.

'Please try to imagine a guy who spends his spare time knocking camels down in a private zoo.'

Karmen was intrigued: 'Wow!' she exclaimed, looking at the man on the business card riding a bison at an undoubtedly furious gallop. There were cactuses around which could have been artificial, as, indeed, could the blue sky background.

'That's with a bison, then,' Sabina explained, turning the card over. It was decorated with a border in the traditional pattern. 'And this is a photograph with a camel!' The same man, but now in khaki trousers and visibly puffing out his chest, was posing with one foot on the prone form of a desert camel which gave no sign of life.

'He's not bad, otherwise, I mean as a man, only a bit… a bit…'

'A bit… hard?' Karmen helped as best she could.

'Maybe not so much hard, as… as…' Sabina snapped her

fingers as she searched for the right word.

'Benighted? Stupid? Primitive?'

Sabina agreed in principle, but she wasn't altogether satisfied. That surprising, quite new kind of manager seemed to require a more exhaustive elaboration for which Sabina did not have the energy just then.

She exhaled uneasily. Her eardrums were buzzing from a sudden change of pressure.

Finally she confessed to her cousin that she had been struggling with a chill on her bladder for days, but that at work she was on the whole able to cope, to hang on until the break when most people went out of the building, for a bun and half an hour's air.

'You probably understand that I want to be as unobtrusive as possible as long as the first wave lasts ...'

Karmen nodded. 'Of course,' she said, as though she understood her cousin's strategy of moving around the firm in this specific phase of her life.

'But today,' Sabina burst out, 'the pressure was so bad down below that I honestly thought I would burst! And then I told myself: bloody hell, what, why and for whom? Am I supposed to pee in my pants just because my husband's run off with some male swine, possibly even worse than him, if that's at all possible?'

Karmen put her hand soothingly over her cousin's cold one.

'And so I headed for the toilet ...' Sabina had hunched up, as though she wanted to drive away the very thought of that walk with a full bladder. And then, not herself knowing why, she gave a brief description of the redesigned part of the building in the American open-plan style, followed by a series of separate offices for the barely mobile top personnel, with fake marble toilets.

She explained that she had intended just to slip inside. And relieve herself, of course. But then, with her hand on the door handle, she was stopped by the voice of the director in the office opposite. She remembered that he had been slowly gnawing on the earpiece of his spectacles and that a spider's web of saliva was glinting ominously in the corner of his mouth.

'He thrust his face into mine, ordered me to blow out and began to sniff my breath, then he grabbed my fingers and sniffed them too, smelling my sleeves, and my collar – disgusting.'

'Does he suspect you again?'

'Not just me. Now he comes bursting into offices and carries out raids, he searches people and turns out the pockets of their coats, he frisks us with his enormous hands and all with the excuse that the whole building stinks of cigarette smoke.'

'Heavens, he ought to be reported.'

'I wanted to tell him that I had to go, but this time he seemed to smell nicotine and wouldn't let me leave, and those crazy eyes of his were almost popping out of his head. It was only then that I realised I was leaking…'

Karmen took hold of her cousin's lower arms.

'A warmth between my legs,' said Sabina. 'Then a flow like a shower.' She tried to conjure up succinctly the moment of letting go in the director's office.

She blew a lock of hair from her forehead and made an unexpectedly stupid face: 'Well,' she remembered then, 'at least I offered to restore everything to its former state.'

For a moment or two they both focused on the business card. The rush was long over and there were only a few students left in the bar.

Karmen was the first to crack up, while Sabina, as though she were changing gear on the spot, first rolled her eyes over the ceiling in an almost demure, religious trance, although it was clear that she could not hold out for long. She grabbed her nose, which immediately ran, and then her eyes filled with tears and soon laughter was shaking her whole body and veins started to stand out all over her while the waiter, hovering over them, collected their empty cups irritably. Their chins were virtually on the table in a vain endeavour to calm the attacks of laughter. Finally the waiter turned away without a word and Sabina watched him all the way to the counter, her eyes brimming with tears.

'Just look at the way that lad minces.' Sabina squinted wickedly, and then, lowering her voice, she added: 'Either there are more and more of them or they've been well scattered...' She put the business card back in her wallet, but her flat chest was still heaving with the remaining laughter in her lungs.

Sabina believed that it was healthy to be driving herself at a generally fast tempo. Above all, she wanted to spend as much time as possible with the boys. She taught them simple card games, threw junior darts with them and made real efforts with table football. She secretly hoped to be able to replace their father if she really put her mind to it. And every day there had to be a proper hot meal, especially at the weekend when all those jobs she had put off during the week caught up with her. She was a small, wiry, nimble little woman, which certainly helped her during this phase of her life.

Although in the first onrush of fury she had thrown the majority of his things out in black bin bags, it was still possible to come across the odd trace of her husband in drawers – a calculator, a lighter or some silliness such as the blue envelope in which he had brought home his first pay. And yet this hardly upset her, which she attributed to the benign influence of her cousin's proximity.

She had been trying to get her all day on the phone, first for lunch, and then towards evening, increasingly often and agitatedly, letting the phone ring until the connection was cut.

When the children had fallen asleep, she spread the newspaper over the kitchen table and turned the pages aimlessly. She wasn't interested in politics, still less in sport. Besides, weariness had permeated her brain cells and she wanted just to skim through the headlines, but then her attention was drawn to a piece about a gay parade. She took it in at a glance and without a qualm of guilt lit a cigarette. Then she walked through the flat with the newspaper in her hand, swearing a little as she did so, quietly, so as not to wake the children, feeling hot flushes burn her cheeks at almost regular intervals. She took a can of beer out of the fridge and bent over the article again. After the first mouthful she felt a sudden pressure in her bladder, but while she was relieving herself her thoughts kept returning steadily to Karmen.

She dialled her cousin's number, for the nth time, and waited.

'Where on earth is that gadabout?' she growled, banging the receiver down. 'Ungrateful kid!'

She settled down on the balcony, in her corner. She was upset. Her small body was quivering like an overworked muscle. The town below her seemed wild, like a hungry animal, and the feeling that she was unjustly cut off from real life filled her with self-pity.

It must have been past midnight when she heard a key in the lock and then Karmen feeling her way through the flat like a diver in flippers, raising her feet high in a touching effort not to step on the toys spread all over the carpet. From one of the enclosed balconies below came a firm, well-balanced riff. Sabina was observing Karmen over her shoulder. Those large, surprised eyes especially irritated her this evening. She concluded that she must be drunk.

'Am I under surveillance here?' she snapped from her corner. 'Yes, yes,' she snorted at her cousin, 'I've got varicose veins, my hair's all broken ends, and I stopped going to the chiropodist ages ago. You may freely convey to our dear relatives what state their precious Sabina is in...'

Her cousin's silhouette shifted in the darkness and the next instant she was crouching by her feet. Sabina ignored her, tapping her foot in the rhythm of the wild electric guitar which she had considered a part of her youth.

'And I'm a terrible mother...' she added, enjoying herself and removing Karmen's hand from her knee.

But Karmen was undeterred. 'Down there, in the family...' she began slowly, at which Sabina suddenly flared:

'"Down there", "down there",' she hissed, imitating her cousin's homely pronunciation. 'I'm allergic to that expression! Please, avoid it in my company.'

'OK, at home, does that suit you better?'

Sabina moved her head back into the deeper darkness. Currents of air from the seventh floor dispersed the background sound of the guitar. A night wind was getting up. Karmen quickly composed herself, and it occurred to Sabina that this little woman actually had a mission in her home.

'Whenever people start talking about which of us has really made it, everyone always agrees that it is you. They say: "our Sabina" or: "our little relative in the big city", in exactly those words.'

This was too much for Sabina: 'Is that what they say?' she asked in a dangerous voice.

'Uh-huh. There's no large family gathering where you are not mentioned.'

'And do you have any idea what's in my job description?' Sabina interrupted her sharply, and without waiting for an answer she snapped: 'This is me, specialist in one kind of product, the taster with the longest experience, an official person on whose palate the whole national coffee industry used to depend! Do you "down there" have the slightest idea how many bloody coffees I've had to swallow in the course of my career? What do you think, where did my stomach ulcer come from? You must surely have heard of the water in which a black man washed his feet.'

After a few tense drags on her cigarette, she extinguished it in her bottle.

'All those little cups of espresso...' She sighed, gazing at the twinkling points of the metropolis. 'With no sugar, no milk, no cream, just black, black, from edge to edge, just as it is, on its own and unadulterated!'

She drew her sunken cheeks through her hands, and then, surfacing, she went on in a tamer tone: 'I was a lioness at work while you were still piddling in the sand, my dear. The whole coffee industry trembled before me. I had the authority to stop production. They called me the Black Queen, you probably see why.' She sighed again. 'And then along came these private roasting plants, they began springing up everywhere, there were more and more of them, and I had to work overtime so that we could retain our monopoly in the new situation.' She shook her head at the thought of the reduced market. 'Don't think I'm blaming capitalism for the fact that Danko left me. He certainly didn't become a homosexual overnight, but, I ask you, would he have decided on life with another man under socialism?'

A shadow of her early illness crossed Sabina's thin face.

She turned her eyes to Karmen, who had been watching her the whole time, crouching between her legs. The wind was raging in irregular gusts and Sabina thought how good it would be to kiss those young lips.

That night Sabina dreamed of a wedding procession. A standard-bearer was waving a heavy banner with all his strength as he made his way along the winding lanes of the old town. On top of the banner flapped a cockerel with its legs tied together, and its feathers fluttered over the straggling procession. The young couple kissed as they trod over the steep cobbles, and then the photographer shouted: 'Cheese!' and the groom turned towards the camera. She recognised her husband and opened her eyes.

The sun was pouring crazily through the windows.

From the other side of the double bed Karmen was smiling at her. She was dressed in her kimono with the water lily pattern.

'Breakfast,' she whispered, with her lips on Sabina's eye.

'You know,' said Sabina then, 'I've decided to go after all! In fact, we could all go together, make it an outing. You said yourself that these are the last nice days.'

'Have you really thought about it?' asked Karmen.

'Lately I've not been thinking but deciding. According to my heart.'

'*Fantastico!*' exclaimed Karmen. 'So, we're going to the parade!'

Sabina was very quickly shaken awake by the synchronised movements with which Karmen handed the boys slices of bread: everything went smoothly, and as though of its own accord, very precisely and without undue expense of energy. Looking on from the side, to start with Sabina believed there must be some secret principles on which this harmony at the table rested. She was genuinely surprised at her cousin's masterful style, and when she was handed her plate she felt as though she had been imperceptibly drawn into a functioning organism. She caught herself obediently waiting for her slices of buttered bread.

That self-explanatory rhythm of breakfast was carried over into the rest of the morning. Karmen resolved problems as they occurred, efficiently, with her limbs; she reached everywhere and settled things at just the right moment, and when the time came to leave, the boys obediently thrust their arms into the sleeves of their little coats, laced their shoes and without much protest agreed to blow their noses.

They parked the car within reach of the centre of town. Each of them sat one of the boys on their shoulders. Gigo did better than Mičko because Karmen was holding him at her height of five foot eight above the ground, which was at least five inches higher than Mičko's position on his mother's shoulders, where, to make matters worse, those small but sharp bones of Sabina's rubbed him.

Their attention was drawn by the first swear words coming from the group standing next to the road. Sabina paused briefly; her breathing was shallow. She coughed. At that moment someone stood on her sneaker, and a little further on a shaved head reflected the strong midday light. A clock struck twelve.

'Shall we get a bit out of the way?' Sabina looked around the square. There were more and more people. She saw Karmen ambling callously about and Gigo sticking up high above the crowd in his Michael Jordan T-shirt. The man in front of Sabina then pulled energetically on the zipper of his jacket and shoved both hands into his pockets. She glanced with interest at his sharp shoulder blades pressing against the jacket.

'What can you see?' she asked Mičko. 'Can you see anything?'

Surrounded by tall shoulders, she decided to rest her eyes on the ethereally blue sky and so, her thoughts wandering, she allowed herself to be alarmed by the fluttering of pigeon's wings from a nearby roof. A little later, the combined energy of the hoarse voices had her lurching dangerously, and when someone hit her on the chin it made that Saturday morning seem still more dazzling. Then she realised it was Mičko's elbow and that he was twisting about up there like a rider who had been assigned the worst mare; she began to think seriously about manoeuvring towards the nearest piece of open ground when she deciphered Mičko's voice through the clamour.

'Daddy!' he shouted, spurring her on with his legs. 'Daddy!'

With the last atoms of her strength, Sabina stood on the tips of her Shanghai sneakers. She pushed past someone's shoulders and thrust her head through a gap between the dark jackets. She saw him stepping out in the very dense leading group. Everything about him was tense, even his biceps under his tight V-neck top. She noticed his quite spare figure, as though he were exercising or – she thought – over-exerting himself. That thought subdued her, but Mičko's voice was beginning to drive her mad.

She realised that she was walking along the edge of the pavement beside the leaders of the procession and she took a firmer hold of the boy's hands. She tried to read the slogan on her husband's black top, but she had never had much grasp of those militant phrases, just how little she realised now, increasingly conscious of her strained spine, which was seriously close to collapse.

Somewhere a siren blared.

In a risky move, she lowered Mičko to the pavement, but his arms were still round her neck. He wanted to be back up there. His lips were moist. A kind of ferocity blazed from his eyes.

'Calm down.' She tried to outshout him. The noise was deafening on all sides. She took his cheeks between her hands. Mičko's eyes stood out and he wanted to get some other words out, but Sabina merely increased the pressure, repeating, through her teeth: 'Hush, hush…'

The voices round about seemed to fade away. All she could hear was Mičko's pulse: 'Ta-dum, ta-dum.'

And then suddenly she remembered the umbilical cord.

Which breaks.

And separates.

Disappears.

Karmen wrenched Sabina's hands from the child's face, leaving the dark red imprints of his mother's fingers on Mičko's cheeks. The crowd was slowly dispersing, and discarded packaging rolled lazily round their feet. Sabina took her son by the hand and he began to drag his feet, deliberately slowing her down. She bent down over his face and whispered threateningly: 'I'll shut the curtains in your room, turn out all the lights and you will beg me to open the door, but I won't, I swear, I won't! No way!'

When they reached the car she caught Mičko exchanging secret glances with Karmen and that further enraged her.

'Get in, quickly.' She pushed him into the back seat and slammed the door. Without a word, she let her cousin take the wheel. She sat down and waited, her eyes half closed, for Karmen to

The last stretch of the way

start the engine. She was actually regretting having let her drive: that constant jerking in low gears: stop – start – stop – then start again. She felt powerless to control the children's unruliness and she put up with their blows through the back of the passenger seat in silence. When they climbed up to the flat the day suddenly lost the polished shine it had had a little while earlier.

Sabina rushed straight to the bathroom. Mičko and Gigo continued their game in the living room. While she was relieving herself, she recognised the sound of the coffee table being knocked on to its side.

'To the barricades!' It was Gigo's voice. 'Chaaaarge!'

She concluded that the mop handle had just hit the partition wall.

She lowered her head on to her bare thighs, expecting Mičko's counter-attack. She was convinced that retaliation would follow. And she sat there waiting, but nothing was happening in the living room. She flushed the toilet and pulled up her trousers thoughtfully. She peered round the door – the living room was empty, but everywhere there were traces of the violent game. The sounds from the children's room gradually died down and Sabina thought how nice it would be if Karmen moved into the flat. As she passed, she touched several jugs of dried flowers. Her heart was beating hard. She heard Karmen slipping quietly over the tiles, crouching down in the narrow corridor to put on her shoes. The sound of the silk lining of her jacket told her that she was just putting it on and she tried to visualise that movement when she tossed back her hair. She hurried into the corridor.

'You've got someone, haven't you?' Sabina was surprised at her own aggressive tone. She caught sight of her reflection in the mirror and thought how unworthy she was of this beautiful creature in the half-darkness. She felt her cousin's slender fingers tickling the back of her neck.

'Oh, I'm in love, and how,' whispered Karmen, 'like never in my life.' A smile hovered over her face.

'With a man?' Sabina burst out to her surprise.

Karmen kissed her cheek. 'Of course. He's from down our way, you'll meet him soon,' she said. 'He's completely ordinary, unassuming and natural.' She glanced at the kitchen clock. 'Christ, I'm late.' She sped out to the stairs and Sabina waited to switch on the stair light before she closed the door.

The radio was announcing that another gay parade had passed peacefully and without serious incident, which was the end of the local and international news. Swallowing a deadly dose of medicines, Sabina could still clearly hear the reports about the weather, the river levels and state of traffic on the roads, although that no longer needed to concern her at all.

The Knights of Zagreb

Nicholas Blincoe

I met Yuri in Gaza city, at the opening ceremony of Palestinian National Television. This was in the garage below Chairman Arafat's mansion. It all seems a long time ago now, though it is only six or seven years. At the time I was with the World Bank and Yuri was working at the Russian embassy in Tel Aviv. Since then, we have both gone through big career changes. I needed to spend more time in England, and so I became a financial journalist. Yuri needed to earn more money, so he left the diplomatic service and took a contract with the United Nations administration in Bosnia. That is a terrible job, believe me, but Yuri is a single parent with a fourteen-year-old son at an English boarding school. He has to make the fees each term.

My son is almost the same age, and also at private school, though this was his mother's decision. Evan lives in Coventry with Sally and her husband, and I see him on long weekends and holidays. Although I moved back to England to be closer to him, we seem to spend all our time together in foreign countries – wherever the low-cost airlines want to take us.

A case in point: a nineteenth-century Viennese-style hotel in Zagreb, the capital of Croatia.

The choice of destination was pure Yuri. We still exchange e-mails fairly regularly, and when I mentioned I was looking for a cheapish weekend break, he wrote to say he was spending the holidays in Zagreb with Misha, his son: would it be a conducive plan to hook up, the four of us together? A week later, I was running around London, collecting Misha from Waterloo station, Evan from Euston and getting us all to Stansted airport via Liverpool Street. Yuri met us at Zagreb airport in a UN Landcruiser. This was eight o'clock at night and I was already exhausted. When Yuri told us he had good news and bad news, I admit I expected something seriously askew. The bad news, we would all be sharing together. The good news, he had booked us into the presidential suite.

The presidential suite, even at a knock-down price and with communist-era plumbing, is still very impressive. There are three bedrooms, a large salon and a smaller study with a PC and an Internet connection. We asked the hotel to put a Z-bed in the study, and Yuri told Misha that was where he was sleeping.

We make the oddest pseudo-family unit. Yuri is basically a soldier: military school, army, picked for spy school and then the diplomatic service, now with the UN. I guess I am an academic: graduate school, World Bank, now a journalist planning a book on the rise and fall of neo-liberal economic theory. Actually, as I write our CVs, I see there is a similarity: we both spent our entire lives in the public sector, in schools and in government jobs, within NGOs and international bodies. My knowledge of business is entirely voyeuristic and theoretical. Unless Yuri has undergone a personality transformation and taken up smuggling or prostitution – still the growth areas in Bosnia, I hear – he knows even less about the business world than I do.

Our sons are more different. Misha is incredibly tall and awkward, with some acne problems and strident opinions on everything. Evan is average height, monosyllabic but with a measure of urban cool. This is not a fond father speaking, I know that urban cool is not a universal currency. But I imagine it plays well in Coventry, even at private school. And I am certain that Misha has a rotten time at his public school. He complains that he is surrounded by idiots.

'Do you tell them that?'

'Of course I tell them.'

'What do they say?'

'They call me Commie, because I was born in Russia. Or they call me Psycho.'

I know I shouldn't ask. But I do. 'Why do they call you Psycho?'

'Because I lose my temper.'

I shoot Evan a look, praying that he doesn't do anything to annoy this angry, gangling geek. A geek with a punch. At that moment, Yuri comes out of the bathroom, shrugging as he tells us he cannot do anything about the noise.

'Let us agree now. If we use the toilet at night, we don't flush until the morning. You understand that, Misha?'

'Of course I understand it. I'm not stupid.'

So the holiday begins.

The toilet hisses and fills and empties and gurgles: imagine a North Korean water-cooled nuclear reactor, in typhoon season. It is three o'clock in the morning when I pull on a T-shirt and trousers and patter through to our presidential salon. I stare out over Zagreb: the moon is almost full, lighting up the grey stone of the Austrian quarter, all chunky square buildings and boulevards striped with shadows and crossed with tram lines. I look at it for ten minutes and decide there is no chance of me falling asleep in the next few hours, so I return to the bedroom, put on my shoes and go down to ask the porter for directions to a bar.

'Are you in the presidential suite?'

'Yes. But I'm not the President.'

'Who are the other men?'

'The older one's my bodyguard. He's ex-KGB.'

'And the younger men?'

'The tall one is my valet.'

'Valet? What's this?'

'A manservant. Everyone in England has one.'

'No way, mate. I lived in England for six years. I didn't meet anyone with a manservant. What about the other guy?'

I decide to start telling the truth. 'He's my son.'

'Is that right? I like him. I asked what he's listening to on his headphones, he says the Grateful Dead.'

'I'm very proud of him. So what about a bar? A quiet one, I just want to sit and read a book for an hour – no girls, no music. OK?'

The bar is in the corner of what looks like an old public building. I find music and girls inside, but they don't come as a package: it's not a strip club or a brothel. There are blinds on the windows and a mix of old rock tracks on the tape deck. I order a whisky soda, take a table against the back wall and start reading my comic.

The guy sits down and says, 'Ah, English. You speak English?'

I have been reading quietly for about twenty minutes, so I guess I have had my share of peace. As I look up, the comic tilts forwards in my fingers and the front cover falls into the shadows. The man had been trying to read the title but now it is hidden.

'What's that: The légume of … what? The légumes of doom? It's about mutant carrots infected with radioactivity? I love comics, all of them. Superman, Spiderman, Turkman.'

'It's league, not légume. The *League of Extraordinary Gentlemen*.' I lift the cover up, so he can see for himself. 'I brought a novel with me but ended up hating it, so I borrowed this off my son. It's about a group of Victorian literary superheroes, like the Fabulous Four or the Justice League of America.'

'I think that's Fantastic Four, my friend, unless you read the queer version.' He clicked his fingers towards the barman, signalling 'two the same', before turning back to me. 'You don't mind if I join you. I remember I read about this League of Extraordinary Gentlemen in a film magazine and it set me thinking, you know. Ideas, ideas, ideas. You can't bottle them, but if you're smart, maybe they're worth something. My name is Djuro, by the way. Remind me, the Extraordinary Gentlemen, yeah? Who you got? Captain Nemo and Jekyll and Hyde?'

'The Invisible Man, Allan Quartermain and Mina Murray.'

'I never heard of Quartermain,' he said, lifting the two whisky sodas off the waiter's tray. 'And Miss Mina Murray is no gentleman.'

'No. She's a vampire. *Salut.*' We lift our glasses to each other and once the whisky has settled in our stomachs we start talking. I say, 'You know what's odd: that I used to read Alan Moore's comics at the age my son is now. I used to read Judge Dredd, remember him? The idea that Evan reads the same guy twenty-five years later, it's as though time has stopped, there's no progress any more. Even the music he listens to is twenty and thirty years old.'

'If something's a classic, then it's a classic. And maybe Alan Moore gets better with every passing year.'

'I don't know. Maybe if I compared Judge Dredd and League of Extraordinary Gentlemen side by side, I would see a development. But I don't know, they seem on a par. What was your idea? Was it for a comic book?'

'Oh yeah. My idea. I want to call it *The Knights of Zagreb*: four guys with superpowers and they're all from Zagreb.'

'Is this going to be a story about Zrinski and Frankopan?'

Ðuro laughs. 'You did the museum tour already? But no. Forget about Zrinski and Frankopan. My idea, we concentrate on the villains, not on the heroes. *The League of Extraordinary Villainy*. Or my original title, *The Knights of Zagreb*.'

'Who are the villains?'

'Number one, I think… have you seen the film *The Usual Suspects*? The villain is named Keyser Soze, and he comes from the Balkans. After his family is raped and murdered, he is transformed into the Devil. And, as the poster says, his greatest trick is to persuade the world that he does not exist. So, again, number one, I would take him: Keyser Soze.'

'Is that a Croatian name?'

'Are you serious? It's a fake name. Like a *nom de guerre*. Like my second knight. His name is Dimitrios, which might be Greek. Or maybe Dima, which could make him Serbian. Or maybe he's from some place like Anatolia, with a Russian father. Whatever. I don't know if you ever heard of him, he's in a movie called *The Mask of Dimitrios*, a black-and-white film with the same cast as *The Maltese Falcon*. They left out Humphrey Bogart, but almost everyone else is there. Dimitrios is a mystery criminal with hundreds of names but none of them real. He may be dead, he may be alive, no one knows. There are only the stories, as he roams the world committing different crimes. In the film, he comes to Zagreb to kill a guy.'

'So Dimitrios and Keyser Soze. Who else?' Then I remember the American TV programme that finished the previous week. 'What about the terrorist guy from *24*?'

'You're reading my mind. What is that guy's name, anyway?'

'Well, it's Dennis Hopper, but I can't remember the character's name. I'll look it up when I get back to the hotel.'

'So you're interested?'

'What do you mean, interested? I wouldn't say I'm bored.'

'Are you interested enough to invest in the concept?'

'Sure. I'll write you a cheque from the Bank of Broken Dreams.'

When I get back to the suite, Misha is awake and on the computer. I ask whether he can look up the website for *24* and, looking over his shoulder, read that Dennis Hopper plays Victor Dražen, a man who 'by all accounts does not exist'. The main criteria for a Balkan villain seem to be a pseudonym, a mysterious background and the possibility that the character does not exist: Keyser Soze, Dimitrios and now Victor Dražen. The perfect addition to the Knights of Zagreb.

The Knights of Zagreb

I go to bed and soon I'm dreaming about the league and the kind of villainy they could get up to.

As we go down to breakfast the next morning, Yuri tells me that he feels as though the staff are staring at us.

I shrug. 'We're in the presidential suite. We're going to attract a certain amount of attention.'

'I told them we were nothing special. Just a group of friends on holiday.'

'But then I told them you were my bodyguard.' I hand him my sunglasses. 'Can you put these on and try and look tough?'

Yuri takes the glasses, telling me they're better than his anyway. Misha and Evan are ahead of us, talking together and getting along better than I ever expected. We are going to have breakfast in an Austrian-style coffee house – Yuri swears it is the best place in Zagreb. We cross a main street, out of shadows and into bright sunlight. There is a moment when the boys disappear into the whiteness, and as the contrast returns the whole world has changed. Armed police block the road.

There has been a bank robbery – we missed it by ten minutes. Yuri soon has all the details: there were three men armed with assault rifles and a fourth man drove the getaway car: a Landcruiser. Yuri nods his head. 'Good car.' The UN loves these four-wheel-drives so much they buy them by the thousand. Clearly they are also useful in Zagrebian bank robberies because the thieves got clean away. They just smashed through the traffic, putting several drivers of smaller cars in hospital. No one had been killed, but it was apparently a savage robbery. Aside from the traffic accidents, a guard had been beaten unconscious.

That night, I sit in the bar in the corner with Ðuro and he tells me that such a well-organised job could only have been carried out by the Knights of Zagreb.

I say, 'They're not real, you know.'

'But the organisation and the execution, they were absolutely perfect. These were not ordinary criminals.'

'You invented the Knights of Zagreb yesterday, to try and prise money out of me.'

'Fine. I'm not saying you have to believe me.'

'And there were four of them anyway. You only have three men in the Knights of Zagreb.'

'No. There are four. I just didn't mention the last guy yet. The driver.'

'The driver? Please. Which one is he? The super-villain with the power to use a stick shift in tense situations?'

'Evel Knievel.'

That shuts me up. For about three seconds. 'Was Evel Knievel from Zagreb?'

Đuro shrugs. 'What do you think?'

'Is that the rule? If they have a ridiculous name, then they come from the Balkans?'

'Hey, I don't invent the names. What do I know? I'm just from Zagreb. It's English and American and French guys who make up these characters.'

'Aha.' I feel as if I have just won a point. 'You admit they're fictional. So how did they rob a bank today?'

I lose my key some time during the night. It is too late to knock and risk waking everyone up: although I'm sure that Misha will be on the computer. I take the elevator back down to reception and ask the night porter to let me in with the master key. As he returns upstairs with me, he asks why I don't wake up my valet.

'What else is he there for?'

'I'm scared of him. Scared to wake him. Scared to sack him. We call him Psycho.'

'Get your bodyguard to take him out.' The night porter mimes cocking a gun.

'Good idea.'

The suite is dark and I go to bed without switching the light on. I drank four large whiskies in the bar and I sleep so well that I am groggy when Yuri comes in and begins questioning me about the wall safe. Eventually, I understand that the safe is open and our passports have been stolen.

'Where were you last night?'

'In a bar.'

'Did you bring anyone back?'

'Not that I noticed. What are we going to do, call the police?'

The police take a couple of hours to arrive. Two of them interrogate the night porter, while the third policeman slumps against the desk and offers Yuri and me cigarettes. I feel they are wasting their time with the porter: he had a pass key to the room, but only Yuri and I had keys to the safe. If the porter is a suspect at all, it is because he was the man who recommended the bar to me. Who knows, maybe he telephoned ahead, warning them that a fool was heading their way.

Yuri translates the porter's replies for me. 'He says he knows nothing. He thinks it was an inside job.'

The porter is shooting meaningful looks at Misha, who, fortunately, seems to be oblivious.

And that's almost it. The story of Zagreb. The police go through the motions, even questioning the guy working the bar where I had spent the previous two nights. Yuri tells me that the barman recognises my face but doesn't recall that I had any drinking companions. I was just a lonely drunk. I could complain, but true or not, his story brings the investigation to a close.

The next day, we visit the police station and the police provide us with an incident report. Evan and I will apply for replacement passports when we return to the UK. Yuri calls a friend in the Russian embassy in Belgrade and has replacement Russian passports

Fed–Exed to the hotel by the morning.

Our flight tickets can only be reissued at the airport. Apparently, it's no problem, we need only turn up an hour early. Yuri drives us in the Landcruiser and tells us he will wait until we are safely on our way back to Britain. The woman at the airline desk accepts my credit card as proof of identity and, while new tickets are being printed, she hands me an envelope.

'This arrived yesterday, Mr Thin.'

My name is hand written in hurried capitals: James Josef Thin. I think, how odd, to write my full name like that. Even if Joseph is spelled wrong.

I tear open the envelope and inside are rough photocopies of four mugshots, laid out on a sheet together. I recognise Kevin Spacey and Dennis Hopper, photographs taken from their roles in *The Usual Suspects* and *24*, and later learn that the third man is Zachary Scott, the actor who played Dimitrios in *A Coffin for Dimitrios*. The last photograph is mine and underneath, in neat block capitals, is the name Đuro Drušković aka Josef Thin. He has used the photograph from my passport, which I guess is now his passport.

Across the top of the sheet of paper, the words *The Zagrebian Knights* are formed ransom-note-style in letters cut out of a newspaper.

I wonder whether to keep the information to myself but I am the type who would crack under pressure. So as we drink our last Croatian coffees and wait for the boarding information, I show Yuri and our boys the photocopy. Misha wants to go straight back to the police, but I am inclined to forget it. Yuri and Evan both side with me. As I tear *The Knights of Zagreb* into small pieces, Yuri says, 'It's maybe a joke. It's maybe a can of worms. Leave it half open, like that.'

Ultimate fighting

Goran Tribuson

The enormous black metal container that had held the town gas was no longer used for anything, but, like a forgotten rusting monument from the 1950s, it dominated the suburbs, which are still known as the Gasworks. It was nearly two hundred feet high, surrounded by an unstable system of outer columns, which could collapse at any minute, and in it, or at least that's what people said, lived dogs, and sometimes tramps, who managed to bear the stench of gas that had still not entirely evaporated even after all these decades. Along the track below the container stretched an untidy row of small houses, some more dilapidated than the others, workers' cottages, and others, hardly any better, which belonged to the owners of drab suburban tradesmen's shops: metal-workers, cobblers, locksmiths and tyre-repairers. Some of the little streets had still not been tarred, and in others the asphalt had been transformed into a memory of distant times. And down there, behind the old sock factory, whose regular square grey structure could be made out at the place where the meadows and marshes began, some other constructions had sprung up, without permission, built of stolen bricks, discarded tin and corrugated sheeting. And it was precisely here that the magnificent end of the millennium was unfolding, although at first glance it did not look that way.

It was just as though in the meantime time had stood still,

thought Robby Flekač, stopping his ancient Opel, his big rusty ship, a kind of street tanker with German registration plates, in front of the bar he knew so well, which, when he had left this wretched area, some twenty years before, had been called Vuglec. From outside, the bar looked just as dilapidated – it had the same large, unwashed glass wall and dirty door edged with metal strips, like butchers and little mixed goods shops on the edge of town, but under the roof of the porch hung a brand-new neon sign: *Hiroshima.*

Not expecting to stumble on any agreeable memories here, Robby went into the bar and sat down at a table covered with a checked green-and-white tablecloth, so dirty that a careful eye would be able to decipher on it everything that had been eaten and drunk here over the last several months. He was hungry, so he wanted something to eat, and he had a business meeting arranged with the local magnate, a man who had been running the show in this part of town, becoming its real owner, ever since the beginning of the transformation of the Gasworks from an unhealthy socialist environment into healthy competitive capitalism.

The Hiroshima was completely empty, with just one balding man with Mongoloid facial features and a grotesquely long, tapering moustache standing behind the counter. He was lazily and sullenly wiping glasses and talking to a sixty-year-old man in a trench coat, a slightly stooped man who was holding a glass of wine firmly in his right hand, and a fishing rod and a can very limply in his left. Above the dirty counter was a long mural of a rocket, on whose tip was drawn the symbol for radioactivity, like a propeller; on the walls were a few cheaply framed photographs with scenes of the aftermath of an atomic explosion; and in the corner by the coat rack gleamed a pinball machine where a brightly coloured mushroom cloud could be clearly made out, a little stylised, but still disagreeably convincing. Wondering where and when he had last seen a pinball machine, the newcomer glanced towards the bar and cracked his fingers, but the landlord continued calmly wiping glasses as though customers were nothing to do with him.

Interested in the newcomer, or just drawn by a desire to talk to someone while he was drinking, the man in the trench coat detached himself from the bar, came over to Flekač's table, sat down without asking, and put his fishing tackle on a spare chair. Flekač thought he knew him from somewhere, but his brain wasn't functioning all that well. He had passed fifty, entering the age when sclerosis struggles most fiercely with memories in a person's head, he had been away for more than twenty years and, finally, who on earth would remember all those edge-of-town faces, puffy with alcohol and pointlessness?

'Are you Flekač?' asked the man in the trench coat.

Flekač nodded, surprised that anyone recognised him after all.

'That Krešo Flekač who everybody called Delon, who screwed all the women in the Gasworks, before he was put away?'

'No, no!' Flekač defended himself, as though he felt uncomfortable. 'Delon is my brother. He was called that after that French actor ... Alain Delon ...'

'I know that he wasn't called Delon after John Wayne,' said the fisherman caustically. 'So, that's not you? Or, you're not him?'

'No. People used to mix us up all the time. He's three years younger and he's still in Lepoglava jail. And I ... I've spent twenty years in Berlin ... On business ...'

'Business, eh?' The fisherman looked at him ironically, taking off his coat. 'Or maybe you split because of the war with the Serbs? But never mind ... You know, there are a lot of furious husbands who remember such things and who would gladly give you a thrashing.'

'I said I'm not Delon!' Robby was getting angry. 'I don't give a fuck about him! Everyone knows I was in Berlin for twenty years and I never messed with other people's wives!'

'Like hell you didn't! There isn't anyone who hasn't messed

with other people's wives! What would be the use of other people's wives if not for that!'

Strange guy, thought Flekač, but considered it was wiser to let him be. And he was just going to have a bite to eat, and maybe a beer, and then he'd get down to work in the abandoned sock factory.

'What'll you eat, mate? Or drink?' asked the landlord, suddenly materialising at Robby's table.

Robby looked up at him. The old man really did look like those ageing bandits in westerns set in southern Texas and burning with technicolor run riot. A half-breed with grey hair and the expression of a nervous dog that couldn't find a tree to pee on.

'Are we "mates"?' asked Robby, with a certain pedagogical reprimand in his voice.

'Come on, Delon, don't fuck about! What do you want?' said the landlord in an agitated voice, taking a pencil and notebook for orders out of his jacket. As though it were possible here to order anything that couldn't be remembered. 'I've known you ever since you got a beating for hanging around Frölich's daughter. Fuck it, just three days before the girl was supposed to get married. You really always were a rat ...'

'Listen, Cockroach!' the fisherman interrupted him. 'He's not Delon, he's Delon's older brother Robby. Delon's still in the cooler.'

'Robby? Where'd you get that idiotic name? Who on earth is called Robby these days?' The bad-tempered landlord wouldn't give up.

'I'm called Robby because I've always looked like Robert Redford ... a bit ...'

'My arse you do! ... You were probably called Robby because you were a robber as well ... But a lot I care! What'll you have?'

'I want something to eat. Before my business meeting.'

'We've got squid with eggs and sardines with pickle ... and beet with stuffed cutlets, only that's from the day before yesterday ...'

said the landlord, shaking the crumbs from the table with a routine movement.

'Squid with eggs?' asked Robby in surprise. 'I've never heard of that. Are they local, at least?'

'Sure they are,' the landlord grunted gruffly. 'Patagonian. I think they're local there...'

And when Robby declined to eat after all and just ordered a cold beer, the fisherman leaned towards him and began to explain confidentially:

'Cockroach is completely crazy! You remember that the Vuglec was once a good pub? Local wine, blood sausage with cabbage, tripe... Cockroach inherited the place through some strange illegitimate line and completely fucked it up. He offers hideous things like sardines with pickle, maize-shoot juice and all sorts ... But what can you do? There's no choice. Every bar in the district is sick in its own way.'

'So why's he called Cockroach?'

'Can't you see he's crazy about atomic war?' The fisherman flared as though annoyed that it wasn't immediately obvious. 'You see those bombs, rockets, that pinball machine! Fuck it, that's his hobby. Some people collect coins, others like model racing cars, but Cockroach is crazy about an atomic cataclysm! Or nuclear... I don't really know the difference...'

'But what do cockroaches have to do with atomic war?' Robby was still quite reasonably surprised.

'Nothing!' the man with the fishing tackle explained. All those bars evidently meant that he rarely made it to the fishing place on the shore beside the old brickworks. 'He heard on the radio that the only creatures to survive an atomic or nuclear war would be scorpions, and he drove his clients mad for days with this zoological story. But then he goofed, he forgot which creatures were concerned, and began explaining that the only creatures to survive the ultimate cataclysm would be cockroaches. There was nothing for it, they called him Cockroach!'

Robby smiled despite himself, drank some of the beer that the devotee of nuclear apocalypse brought him just then, and noticed a large cockroach crawling over the wooden floor. This wasn't any kind of rarity or hygienic scandal, because all the bars in the suburbs had whole flocks of these creatures which made homes under the wooden floors and lived on scraps or the like. They were black, ugly and disgusting, and it seemed to Flekac that the landlord could be right, and that, as well as scorpions, cockroaches would also survive the final demented clash of world powers. Then he put down his beer, warm and certainly not fresh, and tasting of the pee of someone suffering from kidney disease. In Germany he had barely got by and he couldn't afford expensive things, but the worst Kraut lager was better than this vile brew.

And just as he wanted to ask the landlord what this premature beer that he had poured into his glass was called, the door of the Hiroshima opened and Cimbo appeared – the oldest and perhaps the only friend Flekač had stayed in touch with while he was loafing around all kinds of German towns and their prisons. Cimbo was a lively, round, forty-year-old ball, who always wore a knitted hat with a so-called pompom. People said he didn't take it off even in August, if the summer wasn't excessively hot. Cimbo wasn't too clever – in fact, to be honest, he wasn't clever at all, or more exactly, he was almost proverbially stupid. He thought trams ran on batteries, that the lines and wires were there for the tram driver to report a possible fault in the base; he maintained that a male bee was called a trust; he thought that planes flew because they were made of so-called dur-aluminium which was, apparently, lighter than air; and once he took back a pack of poker cards he had just bought, claiming that there was a printer's error, because they had double pictures on them, many of which were upside down.

'I've sorted it all. Dr Črnko will be here in sixty minutes, or more exactly half an hour. He's interested in the job, he just has to check your validity...'

'Validation?' the man in the trench coat corrected him grumpily.

'Yes, that,' retorted Cimbo, while Flekač shuddered with discomfort. Although he himself didn't quite know what validation was, the word 'verification' didn't appeal to him at all.

Seeing that the landlord was approaching their table, Cimbo raised his hand, like a railway worker stopping a train, and rebuked him sternly:

'Don't mess me around, Cockroach! I don't want anything! The last time I had stomach cramps from your trout with mayonnaise, and everyone says you make the brandy from potatoes.'

And when the grumpy landlord had shrugged his shoulders and returned to the bar, Cimbo leaned towards Flekač and began to whisper in his ear, as though it was something that others weren't to hear:

'I ran into Tromblon and I think you have to be careful. If he's going down one street, you make sure you go down another. When he heard you were here, he said he was going to kill you because you screwed his wife. Twenty years ago, admittedly, but he says it's a wound that doesn't heal just like that...'

'Jesus!' Robby thrust his face into his hands. 'This is driving me crazy. It was Delon who screwed his wife, not me! I have absolutely no idea who that woman is or what she looks like! When's he going to stop confusing me with my idiot brother! Where does this Tromblon work?'

'In the Albanian bakery. He's nearly fifty, but he's stronger than ever. They say he can unload three sacks of flour at a time from a lorry...'

'Wholemeal or plain?' asked the fisherman, then had some more wine, which was already beginning to have an effect.

'Why? Is wholemeal heavier?' exclaimed Cimbo in surprise, but he turned back to Flekač straight away. 'It wouldn't be good for you to run into him. Even if you didn't …'

'I had nothing whatever to do with his wife!' Robby banged the table so hard that Cockroach gave a start and looked up from reading some kind of futurological monograph about total war.

'OK, Robby, OK…' his friend calmed him. 'Now tell me why you've come. What's this business you're going to set up with Črnko?'

And when Robby glanced suspiciously at the angler, who was still sipping his wine, not paying undue attention to their conversation, Cimbo just waved his hand.

'You can talk in front of the Professor! He's one of us!'

The Professor! It suddenly dawned on Robby Flekač and he realised that he had once known this suburban eccentric, who had been reasonably normal until something had happened with his wife. But what was it that happened? Had she left him? Did she die? He simply couldn't remember, and all he was certain about was that this time the ill-fated fingers of his brother Delon were not involved. That is, the woman must have been considerably older than the lover-boy now languishing in jail.

'I've come because of a big business deal that will regenerate this district… a deal that will have a turnover of millions…'

'There never were any millions in this neck of the woods. If there ever was anything, it's all already turned over. Into the pocket of that Dr Črnko of yours…' observed the Professor, but Cimbo simply dismissed his bitterness with a wave of his hand, listening attentively to his friend's story. He may have been the local fool, but even in his head the word 'million' rang with delightful resonances. Where there were millions for others, there was the occasional hundred for him!

'Do you know what K1 is?' Robby asked with the passion with which the last, ultimate, crowning question is asked on television quiz shows.

'Yes,' said Cimbo proudly. 'From crosswords. It's that peak in the

Himalayas, oh ... you know, that ...'

He flailed his hands about and spoke with familiarity, as though they had wandered together through the Himalayas, practising the names of their highest peaks.

'My arse, you know!' snapped Robby. 'K1 is a martial sport which is conquering the world at the moment and attracting the healthiest capital into its orbit. It's a mixture of everything: boxing, karate, kung fu, tae kwan do ...'

'And acupuncture ...' added the Professor, not without irony.

'Bruce Lee ...?' asked the proverbially stupid Cimbo.

But Robby had already acquired the momentum of the enthusiast who believes in all his intentions, and he paid no attention to their remarks.

'It began in Japan, and now it's spreading through the world like wildfire. All you have to do is roll up your sleeves, bend down and pick up cash from the ground. Because otherwise someone else will. There are millions of dollars involved. And it's not only K1, either! A hundred other, similar things are involved, and it all boils down to a savage brawl. "Ultimate fighting", for instance. That's a combination of K1, wrestling and everything else! A fucking dynamic thing. Everything's allowed: punching, kicking, wrestling holds, you can knock your opponent to the ground and shove your knee into his forehead ...'

'Are you allowed that famous kick in the balls?' asked the Professor, staring at his glass. 'That technique has resolved a lot of duels here in the Gasworks.'

'No!' retorted Robby. 'This is a noble sport!'

'So, Robby, you think that this ulti... ulti... that it would go down well here in the Gasworks? Here where everything has always collapsed and died. The last cultural event was when the ensign Opsenica organised festive celebrations for Republic Day, but those celebrations bit the dust along with the whole state ... People here can't spare anything for any kind of production. In half the houses the electricity has been cut off, and the gas would be as well, if only they had any...'

'Cimbo, you're a fool!' Robby reproached him. 'Folk are interested in Croatia, not the fucking Gasworks! It's not the Gasworks that's in integration and all that stuff! Croatia is a propulsive country, on the threshold of Europe, the Nato pact, Unicef... and God knows what else... The lads want...'

'What lads?' the Professor interrupted him, just at the moment when he was running out of material for all this desirable integration. 'There are far too many of these inside and outside benefactors to make a person sleep calmly at night. What lads...'

'What lads! What lads!' Robby repeated angrily, as though the Professor's suspicion offended him. 'I'll tell you what lads! The lads from...'

Then he said something fairly incomprehensible, one could just make out 'martial' and 'federation', but even those terms didn't mean a whole lot to either Cimbo or the Professor. All that could be made out was that it was a matter of some obscure association that gave him the credentials to spread interest for this sporting and above all noble skill throughout Croatia.

If anyone really had given him credentials! It was known that some twenty years ago, in stolen Whirlpool overalls, i.e. with good 'credentials', he had gone round the town and ostensibly serviced domestic machines, but in fact stole programmers, thermal elements and other expensive parts from them for an engineer from the other side of town.

Still, this time, he wouldn't be put off.

'I've got a licence for a new martial association which would cover the whole of south-east Europe. To start with Berlin would supply eighty per cent of the fighters, and by next year I would have the right to the world championship in our style...'

'What, you'd be the world champion?' Cimbo gaped, his lower lip dropped and he looked at his friend in astonishment, while the

Ultimate fighting

Professor just laughed softly.

'Go screw yourself, Cimbo! You never did get the hang of anything! When Ruža with the knockers said she'd do anything for you, you brought her shirts to iron...'

'It's all right for you!' Cimbo was genuinely annoyed. 'You had a mother, there was someone to iron for you... What was I supposed to get her to do? As it was she was lazy and clumsy as hell!'

'OK, OK!' Robby calmed him. 'Of course I wouldn't be the world champion. I would have the discretionary right to fix things so that the champion came from my stable, get it? I've got a fighter's stable in Berlin, I've already got contracts with an Albanian, a Kurd, two Turks...'

'Fuck you! Where did you find Kurds and Turks in Germany!' Cimbo gaped, in simple-minded admiration. 'Ah, you really are a smooth operator!'

'Yes, Turks are a real rarity in Germany,' the Professor added indifferently, and ordered another wine and mineral water. 'And there's so much interest in Kurds that they have to be imported illegally.'

'Really?' Cimbo gaped.

'But that's not the fucking point! I want the world champion to be from here! A Croat, get it?' Robby went on, with patriotic fervour. 'Something like that would really promote our country! World champion in a martial skill that is conquering continent after continent! Do you understand, that's more beneficial for us than the Nobel Prize. It's true that we've already invented a whole mass of stuff for the world. The propelling pencil, and the Biro, the torpedo, the gramophone, some miss or other, and Tesla who invented electricity, and the cigarette holder, you name it... But all of that is nothing compared to the world title...'

'And where does Dr Črnko come into all this?' the Professor suddenly interjected. 'He's seventy years old and a little too old to be world champion in martial arts. In bullshitting and shady deals, maybe… They say he bought the sock factory without any money changing hands, ruined it, drove the workers on to the street and now he's selling an empty building…'

'It's that building I need him for!' said Robby Flekač delightedly. 'I would like him to come into the business with me! I provide the know-how, organisation and fighters, and he the building. There's a big hall there where we can make a ring and auditorium. That's where we'd start with fights, and then spread through town: the Sports Centre, the Cibna Tower, Lisinski Hall, the Matchbox…'

'My arse!' Cimbo interrupted. 'The Matchbox isn't adeq… adag… ade… They wouldn't let you have it!'

'They would, they would! All doors would be open to us if only we were able to dream up a local world champion…'

At that moment the door of the Hiroshima opened and the round, greasy face of a little man with sideburns in his early sixties appeared. This was Dr Črnko, the local king of fraudsters, a man for all seasons and all trades, president of committees, but also smuggler of beef and irradiated milk, patriotic politician and trader in faulty guns, a business magnate dressed in an expensive and tasteless winter coat with a fur collar, in shoes that would not have shamed Al Capone, and with a black briefcase, attached to his right wrist with something that looked like police handcuffs. Among many other things, he was the owner of the failed sock factory of which he had once been the director, and everyone knew that as director he had put the contraction 'Dr' in front of his name, which with time became the title of 'doctor'.

With the confidence of a businessman for whom all legal, and also illegal, transactions went smoothly, Črnko pointed at Robby Flekač and asked him sternly:

'You're that Delon who wants to talk about the sock factory?'

'Delon's in jail. I'm his brother…' Robby replied, a little timidly. 'I would like to talk about that sock factory…'

'All right, but if you try to take me for a ride you'll end up in jail yourself!' replied the sham doctor, slamming the Hiroshima door before Cockroach was able to offer him any of his specialities. Mussels with pea salad, for instance.

Some ten minutes later, both of them serious, restrained and sullen, Robby Flekač and Dr Črnko were walking through the large hall of the abandoned sock factory. Production lines, shelves, machines, packing points, where hundreds of women workers once sat, all of that had been loaded on to trucks, taken off somewhere and sold for peanuts, so that the vast space was empty and almost ready, with a few adaptations, to be transformed into a centre for 'ultimate fighting' with a raised ring and an auditorium of a quite respectable size. And while the Professor, with his trench coat, fishing tackle and no doubt also cirrhosis, remained in the Hiroshima, the obtuse Cimbo had scuttled after the two business partners, trying to make out how the conversation was going and what kind of outcome could be expected.

'To be quite honest, I don't believe in this business,' Črnko explained, treading firmly over the wooden floor where the occasional leftover sock and pieces of packaging could be seen. 'Our people work their socks off, in the evening they get a film out of the video shop and then fall asleep after the credits. Or, if they haven't got the cash for a video, they screw their wives for entertainment. K1, K15 indeed! Fighting indeed! None of that will work here! The Gasworks is simply soil on which nothing grows, whatever seed you sow, however much you fertilise it! But, if you really want to try, if you believe in this fantasy, I can sell or rent you the hall. At a commercial price, of course!'

'I'd like us to go into this venture together. Fifty-fifty. You provide the hall, I the fighters. This is certain money, it couldn't be more certain! I've got unbelievable fighters! I've got the Steel Kurd, more popularly known as Der Eisenkurd, then the Albanian national champion, Skenderbeg Kid, I've got Suleiman the

Magnificent, and I'm on the way to creating a Croatian world champion! Mr Črnko, I really have a fantastic stable! Believe me!' Robby was almost begging him. 'You simply have to come into this business, because it's the opportunity of the century! Where's your vision?'

'Eh, if only you hadn't mentioned a stable.' Črnko clicked his tongue, then sighed sadly. It was obvious that this had hit a sore spot. 'Last month I did a private deal to buy a stable of thorough-bred horses near Đakovo, not knowing that they were suffering from ungulates' infectious anaemia. They dropped dead on the train to Italy... near Zidani Most... Luckily I'd bought them on a false mortgage... Listen, Mr Flekač, this is my last offer. If you have some kind of stable of whores for striptease, or to entertain, escort or serve working men, in that case perhaps we could have talked about going into business together. If not, then I can offer you the hall for a million marks...'

'That's five hundred thousand euros,' observed Cimbo stupidly and inappropriately. He had been trotting along behind them like a little boy the whole time; now Flekač gave him a reproachful glance, as though he wanted to say that this really wasn't the right moment for a maths lesson.

'Besides' – the so-called doctor had not finished – 'I've checked your validation and I can't say the results are encouraging. You don't possess any kind of account here, no kind of registered activity, you have no good references ...'

'That's all in Germany!' Flekač defended himself.

'Maybe ... but you've got other things there as well. You've got dubious card players hanging round you, you're apparently under threat of deportation, and there's a story going round of embezzle-ment of cash from a former Yugoslav club ...'

And just as Flekač wanted to shout 'Who gives a fuck about Yugoslav clubs and their Greater Serb affairs' the huge metal door of the factory hall burst open with a terrible crash and in the doorway, as in some martial arts film, the powerful, body-built figure of Tromblon, an assistant in the private Šaćiri bakery, appeared. Had it really been a film, Tromblon would have said, with pathos: 'Stranger, my wife was a tender flower whose virginity you plucked before she was twenty. The justice that is about to catch up with you has added interest now!' But it was not a film, and Tromblon's meagre education was made up of second-hand comics about Alan Ford and 'Dylan Dog', sold under the counter in the Gasworks, so that he was not able to do anything but rush in and yell barely articulately:

'Your fucking time's up, Delon!'

Already accustomed to misfortunes arriving unexpectedly and from all directions, Dr Črnko moved swiftly out of the way, Cimbo fell to his knees in fear and surprise, while Flekač wanted to scream that this was all a fatal mistake, and that he was not Delon but his brother, but he simply didn't manage to since the furious baker's assistant began showering him with blows. He hit him with direct boxing blows, caught him agilely with a kick to the head, and then immediately in the side and thighs, and finally grabbed him deftly round the knees, brought him to the ground, sat on his stomach and began to punch his face, skilfully avoiding the hands with which the unfortunate victim tried to defend himself.

As Črnko did not involve himself in things that brought in less than 25 per cent profit, it was left to the feeble Cimbo to try somehow to save his friend from the crazed fighter from the bakery, who was swinging his arms in all directions, delivering blows that could be seen in all martial sports. He hung on to Tromblon's back, trying to grab hold of his arms, and bite his ear, shouting all the while:

'This isn't Delon! He's his brother! He doesn't even know your wife!'

But does it matter who is who, and who is whose brother, when justice is being so sweetly and successfully meted out?

In the end Tromblon did stop, climbed off the battered Flekač, spat to one side, turned and left without a word. But it seemed that he did it not because he was convinced that he had in fact attacked the wrong person, but more because his opponent was incapable of offering real resistance.

And although he had suffered all those blows of hands and feet with astonishing courage, Robby Flekač suddenly crumpled backwards and hit the back of his head on the concrete, and before he lost consciousness he remembered what had happened to the strange Professor. Long before, more than twenty years earlier, the Professor had come home from fishing and found that his wife had run off with the wealthy central-heating engineer, for whom she had been doing the books for quite a long time. All she left was a little note, on which she had written: 'Forgive me, this may be just for this fiscal year, but it could be for good.' After that the Professor turned a bit funny, and increasingly often he would pick up his fishing tackle, visit all the bars on the edge of town, persuading himself, as he made his way back, that he would find his beloved little bookkeeper at home, as in some fairy tale with a happy end.

But when, some half an hour after the terrible martial massacre, they were sitting in the Hiroshima, where Cockroach and Cimbo tried to get Robby Flekač back in shape, the Professor was no longer there. He had probably gone home, hoping to find his wife there, making jam or sweeping the entrance hall, or else he had decided to end it all with cheap wine in one of the neighbouring dives. Cockroach brought clean water in a plastic bowl, and then brandy in half-pint glasses, with which Cimbo disinfected the cuts and contusions on his friend's face, and then tried to bring down the blue bruises with cold water.

Stretched back in a chair, Robby sighed, groaning with pain, particularly when the alcohol was poured over his wounds, and kept gabbling uncontrollably things that Cockroach and Cimbo simply couldn't understand:

Ultimate fighting

'Fuck it, he kicked me in the side with his left foot, then immediately in the thigh with his right, that was like when Okura floored Stelton in the first round... a fantastic blow. And the way he grabbed me round the knees and threw me on to my back, not even big Cerberus would be ashamed of that! And Cerberus has beaten Oyamu three times and Fu Dong once! I'm telling you, the lad's a pure genius! Shame he's not a few years younger!'

And when he somehow pulled himself together after all those blows, he drank up the rest of the disinfecting brandy and asked Cockroach the landlord to bring him writing things.

A moment later, the sullen innkeeper produced a cheap carpenter's pencil and a sheet of memorandum paper, with a stylised mushroom cloud in the top left-hand corner. Robby muttered something angrily, as though that idiotic stylization exasperated him, and then he lowered his head over the paper and began to write.

He wrote for a long, long time, and Cimbo was finding it all idiotic. As a man from the edge of town, he had been present at hundreds of fights and never – but honestly, never – had he seen the guy who had come off worse sit down at a table and attack fucking words. And then, when it seemed that there would be no end to it, Flekač folded the paper twice, held it out to Cimbo and said importantly:

'You'll take it to him and don't come back without a positive answer!'

'Take it to who?' said Cimbo in amazement, as though he had already figured out the answer.

'Him! Tromblon! He's wanking away in that fucking baker's, when he's a pure genius at ultimate fighting. Did you see those blows, that speed, the way he threw himself at my legs? That must make Črnko see the light and spew out cash! He saw him in action!'

He wanted to add that the baker's assistant was a pure crowd-teaser, but he couldn't remember that complicated English phrase.

'Are you sure you aren't a bit...' Cimbo was concerned. 'Maybe you ought to wait and then write... What does he know about K2! What does he know about martial arts! He's made pretzels, rolls, breadsticks, large brown... He'll fuck both me and you to hell!'

'You'll take him an offer he can't refuse!' said Robby Flekač seriously, probably without realising that he was repeating a well-known phrase from a famous film. 'What do they pay him at that baker's?'

'I heard he got three thousand...' Cimbo shrugged his shoulders.

'Offer him five!' Robby said impulsively, and then, when Cimbo had already reached the pub door, he stopped him and said, this time more coolly and sensibly:

'Actually, offer him four... And the title of the first Croatian world champion in the new style.'

The tourist

Toby Litt

The waiter came back, again, and asked whether there was anything more he wanted. 'No,' the tourist said.

'Another boiled egg, perhaps?' asked the waiter.

'No, thank you,' said the tourist.

'Or some more coffee?'

Serving the same meals in the same restaurant for almost twenty-five years, the waiter had gone stir-crazy. The tourist, accurately sensing this, decided not to reply. It made no difference whether he offended the man; he would not be eating in this restaurant again, or staying in the hotel next door. That afternoon, he would check out; by midnight, he would be halfway to somewhere else.

'I'll bring you some more coffee,' said the waiter, indefatigable. He was a grey-haired man in his fifties; his face told a long story, a boring story, a story of boredom and its agonies.

'No,' said the tourist, 'that won't be necessary. The bill, please.'

The waiter simpered, backed away, pirouetted and strode off into the kitchen.

The tourist watched him without curiosity, then turned his full attention back to the map of Zagreb spread out among the breakfast things. Automatically, his hands found his cigarettes, cracked the pack, floated one to his mouth and lit it. With only three hours left in town, he had to make the most of his time.

The tourist, aged about thirty-five, was Caucasian, of average height, with dark hair, brown eyes and unremarkable facial features. He was wearing a white T-shirt, blue linen trousers, a khaki jacket and canvas shoes without socks.

'The bill, sir,' the waiter said, directly into the tourist's left ear. He had gone the long way round, so as to be able to surprise him.

'Don't worry,' said the tourist, 'after a performance like that, you'll get a tip.'

'Thank you,' said the waiter, putting the coffee cup on to the plate beside the eggshells.

'What's your name?' the tourist asked.

The waiter had finished clearing the table, and was halfway to the kitchen before he answered, over his shoulder: 'They call me Dr Jekyll.'

The tourist crumpled the bill and left it on the table, along with a couple of kuna notes, doubling the price of the breakfast. He refolded the map, and, standing up, put it in the side pocket of his jacket.

At reception next door, he told them he would be checking out at midday. He asked them, please, not to service his room before then.

Outside, the day was already hot. The tourist pulled out his dark glasses and put them on. He decided to start with a stroll through a park that he'd seen from the airport taxi, the previous night. Another cigarette accompanied him down Petrinjska and along Hatzova.

As he walked, the smoke rose, and as the smoke rose, he rose with it. His feet ceased to make any noise as they touched the pavement, for they were no longer touching the pavement.

By the time he had reached the park, he was an inch off the ground. There were few people out on the streets, it was a working day, but still he had to be careful. Once in the shade of the avenue of trees, he felt safe.

He floated past a pretty little bandstand, feeling some regret that he would never hear music performed there.

At the top of the park, he stopped to wait for some cars to finish driving past. A child in the back of the last one saw his feet, the gap between them and the ground, and started to scream with excitement. Quickly, he set himself down and crossed the road.

He walked past some shops and out on to a large square with trams, news-stands, advertising hoardings and a dominating equestrian statue. A glance at his map confirmed his direction, and the fact that it was up quite a steep hill. He liked high points as start points.

For a moment the tourist thought about taking a tram, but that was too complicated. He walked diagonally to the top corner of the square and started up a steep, wavy street. There were more shops here, selling chunky jewellery and fashionable-here clothes.

He felt himself lifting with impatience, and had to exert great self-control to stay on the ground.

On reaching another statue, smaller, of George slaying the dragon, he got out his map. A left turn, through a sort of arcade where the first floor of a house was missing, a right and a long straight brought him out into another square. He looked up, and saw the object of his morning's walk: a large church with brightly coloured tiles on the roof. Upon a red, white and blue background, two shields were depicted – the one on the right showed a castle, the left included some smiling bear-heads.

Luckily, the square was entirely unpeopled. Without hesitation, the tourist rose to the top level of the bell tower and set himself down.

Looking out across Zagreb, he was able to see the gap of the square, the green of park, and to pinpoint exactly where his hotel was. 'Time for some sightseeing,' he said to himself.

He turned away from the view and pulled his T-shirt up to his throat. His belly-button started to dilate; now, it was the size of a mouth, now the size of a vagina giving birth, now almost as big as his chest cavity.

The first of his organs to come out were his intestines, small and large. They were desperate to go and have a nice cooling swim in the river. His sphincter detached itself from his anus with a loud pop – not because it couldn't not, but just because it liked making the noise.

'Enjoy yourself,' said the tourist, as the gooey tube extended itself to its full length – a javelin of shit and mucus.

Next came his testes and his penis. They were, as usual, impatient.

'Wait a minute,' he said.

There had been some disagreement, but finally he had resolved the issue. His genitals were fed up with going blindly about, rubbing themselves basically at random against whatever or whoever they could find that felt good. It was their turn to be chaperoned by one of the eyes.

Neither of the eyes particularly wanted to go (their relationship with the penis and its sidekicks had been a long and troubled one), but after some melodramatic rolling about, the left one gave in. The tourist took off his dark glasses; it popped out.

Falling into formation between his testes, the three balls zipped off towards the nearest twenty-four-hour porn cinema.

In very short order, his liver and kidneys – which were insepa-rable – sauntered nonchalantly towards the nearest bar; his spleen headed for some nearby dustbins where it intended to play hide, seek and kill with the rats; his appendix, as usual, unable to decide what to do with itself, skipped off in pursuit of his spleen; his stomach had plans of its own.

The other eyeball slocked from its socket, making room for the brain, which divided into its constituent parts – cerebral cortex, medulla oblongata, etc. - and shimmied out through the eyeholes.

The tourist

They had decided to go, together, to a gallery.

The heart came out next. It was the most mischievous of his internal organs, and he hoped it would not get itself into too much trouble. With a little unnecessary spurt of blood, which almost reached his white T-shirt, the heart blopped away. If it was capable of sniggering as it beat, that's what it was doing.

His lungs took their time. Pretending to flap like the wings of a cauliflower, they rose up, up, up – above the city, to where the light was brightest and the air clearest.

Suddenly, his tongue changed its mind. It wanted to be with the lungs. Dropping down through his chest cavity, it licked his cheek affectionately and then lolloped away.

The tourist's body felt good. He had been left with skin, muscles, skeleton and his dull-but-necessary lymphatic system.

He could feel a gentle breeze tickling along his spine. It was most pleasant.

The tourist's body took off all its clothes, folded them up and put them in the guttering beside the brightly coloured tiles and then lay down to sunbathe for a while.

The reproductive organs were, predictably, the first to get into trouble. With the assistance of the left eye, the penis had had no trouble at all finding a porn cinema that was open. Clinging to the back of an early morning punter, the dangly little group snuck their way in.

Once in the dark of the screening room, they had felt pretty safe. Only two men were there, both sitting towards the back. The penis led them into the second row, where it jammed itself down in the gap between the seats. They were covered with a rough, red material, which chafed. The eye sat down on the shaft of the penis, the testes dangled down beneath it.

What was happening on-screen was hardly surprising, but the penis liked it anyway. Soon, it was rubbing itself forwards and backwards between the seats. If it had been able to, it would have heard the men behind it doing something not dissimilar. The eye was riding the back of the penis as if this were a rodeo; the testes went stiff and started to rise.

Just then, another man entered the screening room, looked around, saw the two men towards the back and decided to head for the front row. The eye spotted him, but the penis was by now well into its stride; it was unstoppable.

Without any lid, the eye could not close itself. It continued to take in images from the screen, and the penis continued to get off on them.

Just as the man put his hands on the armrests and sat himself down, the penis shot its white load. Splat, right on the back of his hand.

Disgusted, the man stood up and looked behind him. Alerted finally by the eye, the penis had managed to pull itself back from between the seats and was now, with the testes, hiding beneath them.

'Did you do that?' asked the man, or words to that effect. 'What about you?'

The penis and testes snuck along beneath the seats, heading for the door.

'I'll fucking kill you, I will,' said the man.

Hearing shouting, the day manager of the cinema came in — and the penis, eye and testes made their escape through the open door.

By this time, the appendix and the spleen had found their way not exactly by sense of smell, but by something like it, to a nice stack of dustbins. The lungs were up above the clouds, floating this way and that. The intestines were disporting themselves with brown and often deformed fish in the river. The liver and kidneys had laid themselves down in a dank cellar, on top of a leaky beer barrel. The stomach was keeping its secret assignation. The movements of the heart were, as usual, obscure and perverse.

The tourist's body kept vague tabs on what was happening. He'd been a little alarmed at what had taken place in the porn cinema, but now that the danger was past his muscles had relaxed again.

The penis had now decided to go and play its favourite game – getting between men and women on crowded public transport, on trams, and going stiff. The eye, reluctantly, had agreed to play lookout.

After half an hour or so, the tourist's body got dressed. It wanted to go back to the park. Listening carefully, it waited until it was pretty sure the square beneath the church was empty, then floated down. Retracing its steps was easy; it sauntered – pretending, with empty skull cavity, to look through its dark glasses into the shop windows.

On the large square, the body lit a cigarette, and hoped that no one would notice the smoke coming out of its ears.

When it reached the park, the body sat down on a delicate wrought-iron bench. It liked to do this. People would often sit beside it, and talk to it. Of course, it didn't understand their language. But they didn't seem to want it to reply, just to be there and, sometimes, now and again, to nod. Occasionally, in other cities they had become angry and it had had to punch them and run away. It found the sound of their voices, particularly the low ones, soothing – they resonated in its chest cavity.

The body could feel the sun through the leaves of the trees. It was as happy as it had been in a long time.

In the middle of the park, in the Strossmayer Gallery, the brain and the right eye were examining an unexceptional crucifixion.

A man with a radio sat down next to the tourist's body. This was even better than usual: music.

The heart, though, was causing trouble. In Catholic countries, the heart had a favourite trick: it followed the faint scent of incense to the biggest church in the vicinity, went inside, found by some strange instinct Jesus Christ, knocked his wooden heart out of the way and sat there in its place, beating, beating.

Sooner or later, one of the pious – usually a widow; this time it was a widow – would come in, look up and discover the miracle. All the heart had to do was wait.

'O Lord, O Lord!' the widow said, and ran away.

Smugly, the heart sat there, safe in the Saviour's bosom.

The widow brought another widow, and another widow came to see what the first two widows were getting so excited about. Rather than running away again, they went down on their knees and started to cross themselves; they muttered prayers, lifted their hands and cried.

The heart took particular pleasure from this part of the trick. It knew that these women, for the rest of their lives, come what may, would be sustained in their faith; they would probably go on talk shows, become minor fanatical celebrities. Their standard of living would improve; they would own televisions with bigger screens.

Eventually, one of them ran off to fetch a priest.

In five minutes, they were back. The priest fell to his knees. The heart beat harder, and wished it had been able to talk.

After praying for a while, and presumably giving thanks to God, the priest stood up and walked away. He was using his mobile phone. Sometimes they called the Vatican directly – asking for the Pope. More often, they speed-dialled their bishop.

By now a medium-sized crowd had gathered. People had been called in from the street. The heart could sense the rustle of genuflections. Occasionally there was an almost orgasmic cry of religious relief or the flash of a camera.

From outside came the sound of sirens. It was time to be off. Wringing a couple of drops of blood out of itself to leave behind, the heart slowly lifted off. There were gasps, there were screams. It rose and rose, towards the roof of the church, and then disappeared behind one of the rafters.

Below, there was mayhem. The heart skipped along the rafters, careful not to be seen.

But to its dismay, and simultaneously to the dismay of the body on the park bench, the heart found it was trapped. The door to the church, through which it had entered, was now shut; there were no gaps in the roof; the door to the bell-tower was locked.

The tourist's body was scared, its skin began to sweat – nothing quite like this had happened before: many times one or other of its organs had been spotted, but that was only by people on their own or in small groups. Never before had they been sighted by a large crowd, or by the police.

The radio man got up and left, taking the music with him.

Action was needed, and quickly. Most of the other organs were called from all directions to rendezvous at the church. The brain and eye, however, returned to the body, annoyed that the heart had cut short their art appreciation.

They had only just squeezed back into the cerebral cavity when the eye spotted the waiter from the restaurant beside the hotel. He was smoking a cigarette, out on his break between servings. The tourist hoped he wouldn't be seen, but the waiter was in desperate search of distraction – and had the fatal habit of never forgetting a face.

'Do you mind?' he asked, when he reached the bench. Without getting a reply, for of course without his lungs and tongue the tourist couldn't speak, the waiter sat down. 'I'm sorry about this morning,' he said. 'Sometimes I take my frustration out on customers. I know I shouldn't, but I do. There was one time …'

Meanwhile, the other organs had rallied to the heart's aid. The left eye had circled over the roof of the church, and confirmed that the door was the only way in or out. The spleen and appendix, carrying the bodies of four recently strangled rats, were hovering high overhead – as were the liver and kidneys, which were pissed and bloated, but unable to piss without the assistance of the penis. The intestines had laid themselves out along the guttering above the entrance to the church. The penis and testes were lying in a heap beside a nearby stall selling magazines, pretending to be something a cat had thrown up.

'And then there was this other time…' the waiter said. The tourist's body nodded. The brain had by now formulated a plan – this it communicated to the waiting organs.

Joining together, the tongue and the lungs went to a point just above the entrance to the church but still out of sight. Once there, they waited for the signal. The other organs took up their positions, too.

The tourist's body stood up from the bench. 'But wait…' said the waiter. 'I haven't finished telling you.'

The body turned, gave an apologetic shrug and gestured towards where its penis would have been.

'Ah,' the waiter said, 'I poured you one too many coffees, didn't I? I apologise.'

The body set off back towards the hotel, the brain sending the go signal.

'If you don't mind,' said the waiter, 'I'll just join you. A sympathetic soul comes along so very infrequently.'

High above the hysterical crowd, the lungs drew breath and the tongue let out a long ululating scream. A few people looked up; the lung-tongue repeated the scream; more looked; they screamed again; soon the whole crowd was staring upwards.

It was a glorious moment – the smaller and larger intestines had been perched ready on the edge of the gutter, and now they voided themselves in a vast splattering arc of faeces. The penis and testes, which had rejoined the liver and kidneys, followed this up with more accurately directed spurts of beery urine. And as if this weren't enough, the spleen and appendix dropped the bodies of the rats.

The crowd panicked. People ran in disgust, away from the church, as fast as they could. The police were carried off with them. 'It is the Devil!' some of the people shouted.

The left eye watched with satisfaction, hovering.

'Sometimes I feel,' said the waiter as they entered the hotel lobby, 'as if I just want to burst.'

The body shook its head, sadly, sympathetically.

Having heard the commotion outside, the crowd in the church wanted to know what was going on. The door opened, just a crack, but it was enough. With the guidance of the eye, the heart was out, off and away – followed by the other organs, now flying in a V formation. One or two people, looking up to heaven, saw them, puked.

The body took the waiter by the hand, squeezed and shook, sincerely. If it had had its tongue with it, it would have told the waiter how it, too, had felt exactly the same, how a few years ago it had felt so bored it could have exploded, and then, one day, how it *had* exploded, and then how it had put itself back together again. But it couldn't. It stepped silently into the lift and pressed the button for the top floor.

Back in the room, the tourist opened his windows wide, pulled up his T-shirt, spread his belly-button and waited for his organs, like slimy homing pigeons, to return from their adventures.

A piece of the moon

Salena Saliva

With a knife in one hand, she has been feeding the muse slices of apple, hunks of cheese, red wine and bitter herbed alcohol, dark as liquorice. There she lay with a young dark Croatian boy wet from the shower, his eyelashes long, black and heavy with water, lips blue with wine, his chewed cigarette butts in the ashtray.

Leila smokes lying on her back on the bed, a white sheet half on the floor.

Her wet hair makes a damp dent in the pillow, she is speaking on the phone.

'... some of the old buildings, like the theatre, are painted this deep dark banana-toffee yellow. There is something about the sun shining through the autumn leaves. When the sun shines through there is this distinct marriage of gold and amber, contrasted by the wintry blue sky, it's truly beautiful... You know, the sky here reminds me of Salzburg, remember Salzburg? Kicking the leaves in the forest by the castle, kicking them at the camera lens and laughing... so drunk on schnapps and, hmmm, ah...'

He's dressed, he has slicked his wet black hair back, he lights a cigarette and looks at her through the blue flame then back at the orange tip. He blows on it to ensure it's lit.

'and... I must go... yes, or I will be late... I will try to call you later... hmmm... 'bye.'

A piece of the moon

'I had better go now, Miss London...' he says, leaning against the wall.

'Yes, and I had better get my act together or I will be late. See you later maybe?'

Leila pulls a black shirt on and buttons it with one hand, pulling back the curtain with the other. She looks down at the busy street below and sees a rose seller, one of his eyes glazed with milk like a piece of the moon. She gets on her knees, looking under the bed for her other boot.

'Yes, maybe. Maybe,' he says coolly, exhaling a billow of smoke, like wind in a sail.

He extinguishes the screwed-up tarry butt in the ashtray. They kiss hurriedly at the door and laugh, whispering again, yes, maybe later, maybe no, maybe, maybe...

Once dressed, hair half dry, she leaves. As she locks the hotel door she looks down to find a dirty brown paper package outside her door, tied up untidily with string, with no clues but her name handwritten in blue capital letters: LEILA GOODMORROW.

The packet must be from him, she assumes. The young lover. And she giggles to herself because, like all girls, Leila loved surprises. It was a rectangular box, the size and shape of a box of tissues, and on shaking it there was no noise. It had a distinct scent of something. For some reason it reminded her of the sound of a clockwork music box she'd once had, with a ballerina that turned slowly whenever you opened it. It had the scent of summer things.

Alone in the mirrored elevator, Leila watches her own reflection stare back at her. She was about to open the package when suddenly the elevator jolted to a standstill. The doors opened automatically. Leila put the packet into her unzipped shoulder bag to free her hands and help to hold the doors open, as a family with three children get in awkwardly with a pushchair. Within seconds the doors open on the ground floor. She had the mystery in her bag, rattling around with her notebook, wallet, pens, poetry books and cigarettes. She hoped it wasn't something that would easily break or that could leak on to her books. In the downstairs lobby café she found her friend Darko, a thick blue cloud of smoke around and above him as he sucked Opatija cigarettes.

He stood tall and bent to kiss her hello, swigged the last of his thick black coffee, and they left to have a late and lazy lunch. It's mid-afternoon. It's a bright blue sky they walk beneath, arm in arm, and a busy Saturday surrounds them.

There are blue trams, newspaper stands, tobacco kiosks and street entertainers. They pass narrow buildings, some with black wrought-iron balconies decorated with red and pink geraniums. A bearded man plays guitar, a folk song nobody seemingly liked, but there were more than just a few coins in his hat. The rose seller, one of his eyes glazed with milk like a piece of the moon, is standing in the square, multicoloured flowers wrapped individually with brown paper, and people pass him by. Leila noticed him smile as if towards her; she looked away and up to see tiny attic windows with old yellowing lace. The trees were in turmeric, saffron and curried yellow, a flock of black birds in a vast swimming-pool blue.

'Autumn is the colour of a tropical beach here. Gold sand-coloured leaves and blue endless sea sky...'

'It is a very beautiful day and, may I say, even more so with your lovely self.'

'Thank you.' She laughed. 'And may I say with you too.'

They take the wooden booth at the back, as was now usual, and order a pair of clear pear brandies chased by Ožujsko beers. It's an old restaurant with black-and-white framed pencil drawings of old Zagreb on the white walls.

'...that is why I find I am sometimes so in love with this life, with this world. I seek evidence of good, of God everywhere...' Leila is saying.

'I seek it in the most ordinary places, in everyday people. On summer days I sometimes take walks in London from Baker Street, past the BBC to Soho. I watch people rushing past me on Oxford Street and I will just stop and stand there, still, by a lamp-post and just listen. I feel like I am collecting evidence and looking for signs, for angels. I suppose it's just trying to live with eyes wide open...'

'Well, you know, London is a very special place for me, I feel lucky there.' Darko's voice is very deep and gentle. He continues after exhaling, lifting his glass, nodding cheers and finishing his brandy in one careful gulp. He says, 'There are devils, why shouldn't there be angels too... maybe we are all a little bit of both, a little good, a little bad. More brandy, Leila?'

'Yes please...'

Darko motions for more drinks to be brought to the table.

'Yes, and you know what, I am utterly convinced that nice people always have bad teeth. Good people always have teeth with character, stained or a bit crooked. I don't trust that perfect white bite.' She bursts out laughing and says: 'Or maybe it's just because skint people don't go to the dentist in England... if at all.'

Leila and Darko grin, baring their teeth at each other while the drinks arrive.

'It's funny, you know, how we all affect each other, one person brings out one part of you and someone else, something else entirely. People stick with you. Real people tattoo you. One day you will be catching a bus and you will get a smile from a stranger that just stays with you...'

She thinks of the rose seller and pushes his memory away uneasily.

'...Or you will be doing something, say, ordering a pizza, and a mannerism, the way you hold the phone, will distinctly remind you of someone. It will be like they are smiling with you, they are with you. It's like people never leave you.'

'Lost friends too, maybe you will dream of them, and it is as though you have been visited by them. I had a friend who died. I often remember him in my dreams... he is with me sometimes, I think.'

The bartender brings them the same again, with slices of *kulen*, dried spiced pork, Livno cheese and bread. They thank him and light cigarettes.

'Here's to old lost friends!'

'To lost old friends and to new old friends.' They laugh and raise glasses.

'To poor and old friends with rubbish teeth and *odjeb*i to dentists!'

'*Odjebi!* Dentists!'

'Dentists *pička*!' laughing at Leila's terrible Croatian swearing.

'You know, I heard about this family of tattoo artists. They were really into the art of it, a whole clan of skilled artists, and one day the mother died and in her will she asked that her ashes be put into the tattooing ink. Imagine that, she lives for ever in the blood and scar tissue of all their customers...'

'I have a huge black pirate's skull and cross-bones across my arse,' says Darko.

Leila chews the cheese thoughtfully. She swallows some beer.

'Really?' She believes him.

Darko is shaking his head and laughing.

A feeling. It reminds her of something, all this talk of angels and teeth and dentists and tattoos and old friends. And then she remembers the package. She had entirely forgotten about it. A bubble of excitement and curiosity.

Time passes quickly, as only good times can and do. The restaurant is busier and noisier now. The people at a table near to them are laughing and eating. A bald man smokes a pipe and a plump lady is being helped with her coat. Her arms are short, her bust heavy and her hair is burnt, pale apricot with a perm.

The bartender cleans the ashtray, the restaurant is vibrating with chatter and smoke.

A piece of the moon

'And now we must leave and go to Klub Gjuro to meet Dražen and Eduard. I am so bloody pissed this is really going to be quite some fucking reading.'

'Tonight… *idemo se razbiti.*'

'Yes, tonight we fucking kill ourselves!' They splutter and laugh, staggering towards Jelačić Square arm in arm. It has been raining and it is already dark. The wet cobbled paving slabs shine. It's a bright starry night and the spirits are high. The world is spinning a little faster. The rose seller, one of his eyes glazed with milk like a piece of the moon, walks towards them. They speak fast in Croatian that Leila doesn't understand. She looks at the street lights reflecting in the pavement and the stars in the sky, anything but at the sad face of the rose seller. Darko buys a rose; he clicks his heels and dips to bow gallantly and gives her the lovely flower, red and dark like wine.

'Thank you, kind sir.' She curtsies jokingly and beams and pokes it through her top lapel buttonhole, then there is that smell again, it reminds her of something.

'What did the rose seller say to you?'

'He was talking about his… Oh, shit… Excuse me, Leila, I must go back to get my books, I fucking left them in the bar. Will you be all right to sit here and wait? There is no reason for you to come all the way back too. Here, smoke; Opatija. This word in Croatian means abbey. OK, wait here.'

Leila smokes, sits on a bench and watches Darko disappear out of sight. She looks up to the stars. The moon is almost full, oval shaped. The air seems clean after the rain. Fresh and chilled.

Leila remembers she is in a foreign country, watches people; pretending to understand their conversations. See the man in the suit, the tip of his umbrella tapping the cobbled stones, talking to the young girl with the uncomfortable heels. He might be saying come back to mine because his wife and children are away on holiday in Split and she is thinking of ways to get out of having to kiss him goodnight. There a gang of young boys laughing excitedly. She decides they are laughing about football.

There, see the rose seller, one of his eyes glazed with milk like a piece of the moon. Now he is by the tobacco kiosk, his coat is ripped and dirty, his shoes are worn with holes, he has only three fingers on one hand, he walks bent and people pass him by. She shivers, then remembers the packet she feels inside her bag. She opens it carefully, unravels the string and then tears into the paper.

And now there she has it, evidence of good, as suddenly as that.

There was no flash of white light, no crescendo of pianos, and it did not start to rain bubbles. No stars collided or rivers burst. Clocks did not stop, time did not stand still.

There were no colours but the oil in the puddles in the gutter.

There was nothing but empty paper in her hands, an empty brown paper box and an overwhelming smell of roses. She looked into the night sky and the moon was now complete, wholly whole. She inhaled and closed her eyes for one moment. It was warm there in the moment, and nourishing. She remembered the sound of a clockwork music box with a ballerina turning slowly whenever she opened it.

Darko was returning with his bag of books. She walked towards him and took his hand. They ran to get on the 14 tram. She looked behind her, through the window, and there saw the rose seller smiling as if towards her. The rose seller. No longer was one of his eyes glazed with milk like a piece of the moon.

Junk food kills, doesn't it?

Jelena Čarija

If this were a screenplay for a film, it would start like this:

EXT. STREET IN FRONT OF THE JUNK FOOD FAST-FOOD
RESTAURANT IN ZAGREB – NIGHT

Two girls get out of a taxi. They are laughing.

*The TALLER one is twenty, has loose red hair and hides her excess
two and a half stone by wearing black clothes and high heels.
The SHORTER one is an exceptionally pretty thirty-year-old. She has
dirty blonde hair, which falls over her large blue knitted shawl. Under the
shawl we can make out the body of Pamela Anderson.*

SHORT
(to the taxi driver, slamming the door of the taxi)
Goodnight!

*The taxi drives off into the night.
Short opens the door of Junk Food and lets Tall go in first.*

INT. JUNK FOOD – CONTINUOUS

*A stereotypical fast-food restaurant with sandwiches, neon lights, non-
alcoholic beverages, ice cream and photographs of famous actors hanging on
the walls. Waiters wearing yellow shirts with the firm's logo. Of the roughly*

fifteen customers, ten are the most typical white trash. We see only one member of the gentler sex, about twenty-five years of age, accompanied by a young man.

Our heroines enter confidently. Under the neon lights we see the remains of their evening make-up. The ten representatives of white trash weigh them up from head to toe. They pass by a waiter and greet him.

SHORT
(quite softly)
Good evening!

The waiter forces himself to respond. He hates his job.

WAITER
Good evening!

They go down the stairs leading to the basement section of Junk Food.

INT. BASEMENT – CONTINUOUS

All the tables, eight of them, are empty. The two of them sit down at a table in a booth opposite the toilets.

They look at the price list and choices.

CLOSE-UP — UNDER THE TABLE

Tall takes off her high heels and stretches her toes.

BACK TO SCENE

TALL
I'm hungry.

SHORT
(with a slight foreign accent)
I'll have a toasted sandwich and a Coke. And a vanilla ice with caramel, maybe.

Junk food kills, doesn't it?

TALL
(looking at the menu)
I'll have… I think I can't see to read at all. I'm drunk.

SHORT
(confidentially)
You're not drunk, my dear, your contact lenses are just too weak.
That's why you can't see.

*They both start laughing. The girls start a conversation with the waiter.
Their voices merge with one another in the lively exchange.*

WAITER
Good evening!

SHORT AND TALL
(together, laughing)
Good evening!

WAITER
(looking down his shirt)
What's funny?

SHORT
(without stopping laughing)
Nothing, we're just having a bit of a laugh.

TALL
There, we'll stop now. She'll have a toasted sandwich, so shall I,
two Cokes …
(looks at Short)
Diet?

*In the background a YOUNG MAN, thirty years old, nearly six feet,
fourteen stone, in a garishly coloured tracksuit, with a thick gold chain
round his neck, comes down the stairs.*

SHORT

Diet? You crazy? Ordinary, regular...

TALL

(holds up two fingers)

Two Cokes...

The Young Man comes up to the table and stands silently beside it. The girls take no notice of him; they think he has come because of the waiter.

TALL

So, two Cokes and ice cream... vanilla with caramel, twice again.

(Looks at Short)

Will two ice creams be enough for us?

SHORT

(in an I've-thought-of-a-clever-solution tone of voice)

Well... two of every kind.

TALL

(to the waiter)

How many kinds of ice cream do you have?

WAITER

Five.

SHORT

(looks at Tall)

Twice five, i.e. ten ice creams!

TALL

(to the waiter)

What kinds are they?

WAITER

Vanilla with caramel, vanilla with chocolate, vanilla with forest fruits, vanilla with lemon cream and vanilla with tropical fruit.

Junk food kills, doesn't it?

SHORT

Bring two of everything.

The waiter looks at them fairly blankly because they've ordered
ten ice creams.

WAITER

Ten ice creams? *Two* of everything?

TALL

(nods yes)

And, oh yes, bring us two Cokes each, we're very thirsty.

(Laughing)

So that you don't have to come *twice*!

The Young Man suddenly joins in the conversation.

YOUNG MAN

(to the girls)

Something's funny?

TALL

No, we're just ordering ice cream.

YOUNG MAN

(ignoring her answer)

So tell me too, *what's* funny?

SHORT

We're just ordering ice cream.

(To the waiter)

So, two toasted sandwiches, four Cokes and ten ice creams,
two of each kind.

WAITER

Very good.

The waiter is about to leave.

TALL
(calls to the waiter; the waiter turns back towards her)
And a glass of water for me!
(looks at Short)
Want one?

SHORT
(directly to the waiter)
A glass of water for me too!

TALL
(to the waiter)
Sorry to be such a nuisance, but we haven't had those eight glasses
you're supposed to drink in a day.

WAITER
(with a smile)
Anything else?

SHORT
No, no, sorry to be a nuisance, that's all, thank you.

The waiter leaves.

YOUNG MAN
(addressing both of them)
Would you like to join me and my mates upstairs?

SHORT
We'd love to, but we're really tired.

YOUNG MAN
But why not? We'd really like you to sit with us. It can't be much
fun for you here on your own.

TALL
No, maybe another time.

Junk food kills, doesn't it?

YOUNG MAN

There won't be another time! I'm here now, I'm going to Holland in two days' time. It's now or never!

SHORT

Sorry, but we really don't feel like company.

YOUNG MAN

(quite agitated by now)

You think I'm some sort of idiot? I earn five hundred marks a day! I'm in the fitness club every day, the whole day, and I have a great life, I'm not an idiot from a building site.

The girls look at each other. Why is he telling them this?
Tall hunches her shoulders.

TALL

You're nice, but we really just want to be alone.

SHORT

(to Tall)

How do you say 'we've got nothing against you' in his language?

TALL

Nothing personal.

SHORT

(looking at the Young Man)

Nothing personal.

YOUNG MAN

I understand what 'having nothing against you' means, but I really don't understand why you don't want to have a drink with us. We're not tramps!

Jelena Čarija

TALL
(jokingly, with a light laugh, looking at the price list again)
We don't like anyone watching us when we're eating.

YOUNG MAN
(in a dangerous voice, to Tall)
Are you laughing at me?

TALL
*(looks at him, confused, apologising – she hadn't expected such
an aggressive tone)*
No, no, forgive me. We're a bit… I'm looking at the ice creams.

Short takes Tall's hand across the table, protectively.

SHORT
We've had a bit to drink and we're having a laugh.

YOUNG MAN
You're having a laugh and you don't want to sit with us?
We haven't got the plague!

SHORT
Look, I've just arrived from Australia, I've been travelling for
twelve hours, this is my niece, we haven't seen each other for
nearly two years, we simply want to be alone for a while, chat and
have a sandwich. Another time…
(shrugs her shoulders)
…with pleasure. But this evening we really want to catch up a
bit, talk about the family and all that, we haven't seen each
other for so long…

The Young Man looks at them, angrily. He rubs his nose on his sleeve.

YOUNG MAN
You're both mental.

Junk food kills, doesn't it?

TALL
We're sorry, don't be angry, but we really don't feel like company.

SHORT
You can see that we came down here, beside the toilets, we simply
want a little privacy.

YOUNG MAN
OK. You're just a pair of sad wankers.

Tall and Short look at each other.

SHORT
Some other time.

*The Young Man moves away from their table. He seems to have
got the message.*
The girls lean across the table towards one another.

TALL
(in a whisper)
What a loser!

SHORT
(in a whisper)
Cocaine addict! You can see it at once!

*Suddenly O.S. the voice of the Young Man talking at the top of his voice
on the first floor.*

YOUNG MAN
They're just two whores, down there. Just great whores!

The girls look at each other, astounded. Had they heard right?
The Young Man keeps on talking.

LOW SHOT
*The Young Man's feet and lower legs reach the floor under a bar stool
by the bar.*

BACK TO SCENE

YOUNG MAN

Two stupid whores! The older one's just about OK, but the younger one keeps tittering like an idiot… but I know what she needs.

(pause)

She needs to be screwed, then wasted!

The fawning, approving laughter of several men.

Short makes a movement as though she is going to get up from the table, but Tall grabs her by the hand.

TALL

(whispering)

Leave him, he's a cretin! He could kill us!

Short struggles out of Tall's hands, which are trying to restrain her across the table, with such force that she pushes the table away and completely alters her expression. She charges upstairs, leaping up them two at a time as though she were flying.

The camera stays downstairs – with Tall. She puts her hands to her head in disbelief. Her expression suggests that she probably thinks she is drunk and that she is imagining everything that is happening and she turns quite ashen.

INT. JUNK FOOD, FIRST FLOOR – BESIDE THE BAR

The customers and the waiter look up inquisitively.

SHORT

(furiously)

Apologise!

YOUNG MAN

(feigning incomprehension; smiling)

Who to?

Junk food kills, doesn't it?

SHORT
(even more furiously)
To my niece! No one fucks with my family! What you said about
my kid, that she had to be screwed then wasted, apologise!

YOUNG MAN
(into her face)
And what will you do to me if I don't, bitch?

Malicious male laughter in the background.

The sound of a powerful slap rends the air.

I stood beside the table, watching part of what was going on
through an opening in the thick blue-painted concrete wall, at the
moment when my aunt gave the guy in the garish tracksuit an
almighty slap, the hardest I had ever seen anyone get slapped in my
life. There was silence in Junk Food. He hit her back. She knocked
him off the bar stool where he was sitting. He fell on to the floor. I
saw her feet wrapping round his neck and kicking him. My aunt's
former husband had been a regional champion in some sort of
martial arts. I saw the flash of astounded looks. That little woman
had knocked that body-built guy to the floor? I know, I look a
huge coward in this story. I remember standing and watching, I
couldn't believe it – this must be that state of shock which follows
immediately after a car accident when you can't believe that you've
had a crash and that your car's a write-off and that you've been
lucky to escape death and that your co-driver's in a coma, and the
passenger in the back seat is dead. I was expecting someone to
react, that a good fairy would prevent this shit with a super-wave of
her magic wand, that some man would get up and say: 'Hey, don't
hit that woman, leave her alone,' or that the waiters would do
something useful. SOMETHING! SOME FUCKING THING!
Didn't the price of toasted sandwiches, Coca-Cola and vanilla ice

cream include some little figure for our safety in this fucking place? I stopped believing in any kind of safety when I saw my aunt sailing through the air. Her body hit the ground, to the right of a circular indent in the wall. The wall shook. I had the feeling that I was going to see pieces of her brain as I climbed up the stairs. I had the feeling that we had accidentally become characters in a Tarantino film.

She is lying on the floor, her spine bent, her head leaning against the Junk Food wall. She is dead. My aunt is dead. My aunt came from Australia to Croatia and was killed the very first evening! My aunt is dead because some shit said he wanted to rape me and kill me! My aunt is lying dead on the floor. Junk food really does kill! Some twenty people are looking on, the waiter's mouth is wide open, the madman and his two friends are standing calmly by, my aunt is lying dead on the floor, no one stirs, as though someone had frozen time, nothing happens, my aunt is lying on the floor, I can't believe she's dead, I met her at the airport today with a bunch of white roses, two minutes ago we ordered sandwiches and Coca-Cola and ten ice creams, and now I'm looking at her corpse! I want to go to her, I want to jump on the man who killed her, but my legs have disappeared somewhere. I'm drunk, I assure myself that this isn't real, they must have put a drug in my drink, I'm hallucinating. My aunt is lying on the floor, dead. This must be a reality show, she can't be dead, although it looks as though her spine has been fractured, although her eyes are closed, although she's not breathing. On the other side of the ring stands the son of a bitch who killed her, watching, looking at the dead body of the woman he had been chatting up a minute before. All the witnesses to the murder are horrified. In their eyes I can see that in court they will say they hadn't seen a thing. My dead aunt opens her eyes. My dead aunt raises herself on to her left arm. My dead aunt gets to her feet with the sudden movement of a cat. My dead aunt turns into a killer tiger. She leaps on to her murderer, the murderer is shocked by the resurrection of the dead woman and the appearance of the tiger, everyone is shocked, I stand on the stairs, I feel myself beginning to cry and I haven't a clue what I'm doing on those stairs, I feel – I should get involved as well, I ought to start beating that vermin, but I can't find my legs, I can't move, something is rooting me to the spot – and my eyes are looking at the most beautiful thing they have seen in their life. I'm looking at a woman who is ready to die just because some cretin said something horrible to me. I'm looking at my aunt's love for me, which has left her body and, as in some myth, turned into a tiger. But I'm not the only one to see it. I know that everyone sees it! All the waiters standing at the bar. All the men in Junk Food who have permitted some jerk weighing fourteen stone to beat up a woman of eight, in front of their very eyes, those dozen big men who allowed my aunt's head to hit the concrete wall. They can all see that tiger. Dear jerks, who approved and grinned, is there anyone who would be prepared to become a tiger for your sake? Is there anyone who would be prepared to hit their head on a concrete wall and die outright? Look, gaze, admire! You have to admire what you haven't got. I see the garish, patterned tracksuit of the guy who I thought had killed my aunt. At this moment I know, he can't kill her! Who could kill a tiger like this? Why had I thought she was dead when I saw her with her eyes closed, after her head had cracked against the wall? Why, he could have been three times six feet tall, he could have weighed three times fourteen stone, he could have had ten times more muscle and a twelve-times-smaller cock – but he could not kill her. My aunt is Artemis, a mythic tiger, Love and Energy. He is shit. Shit cannot kill Artemis, a mythic tiger, Love and Energy. Never.

I'm standing on the stairs. The shit takes my aunt in his arms and throws her. Throws her towards the stairs. The shit really does want to kill my aunt! He throws her at me, because he wants to kill me too! Everyone watches the tiger flying through the air, the tiger

Jelena Čarija

falling at the top of the stairs, the tiger who is going to fall down the stairs, the tiger whose body somersaults, the tiger who is about to break her back on these bloody stairs from the first floor to the basement. My aunt's body hits me in flight, I lose my balance, my body is going backwards, but somehow – I've no idea how – I clutch the banister with my left hand, and with my right I manage to grab her hair… I feel I've grabbed her savagely, I see the skin on the crown of her head bristle as it recoils from my clutch, I feel that my body is crucified between my handhold and clutching her body, I feel that I am crucified on a medieval instrument of torture, I feel happy because I caught her before she broke her neck on the stairs, I try to get my balance, I hug my aunt and look at the shit, who is watching us. His look says he's not used to women fighting back, when he hits them. The shit is scared shitless and leaves. His mates follow him like his henchmen.

My aunt pushed me away from her and headed back up the stairs. I grabbed her. She hit me to make me let go, she shrieked that she was going to find him and kill him, she shrieked that she'd find out what he was called and that he'd die under torture. The shit had disappeared from the scene, I saw him turning to look through the glass door, I heard him quickly starting his car, I could imagine his astounded face, distorted by the fact that he had not managed even to knock an ordinary little woman out, let alone kill her!

'I'll find him,' said my aunt in front of all those people. 'I'll kill him like a little rabbit!'

We looked for her shoes. At that moment, the only girl in Junk Food began crying loudly. She cried for us and for herself – the same thing could have happened to her if she had refused to have a drink with some ugly, unshaven jerk.

And she was crying because at that moment she had realised that her sweetheart was nothing but the most ordinary jerk – he had let all this happen. All girls burst into tears when they realise

Junk food kills, doesn't it?

they are involved with losers.

We didn't dare walk home after all this.

The taxi driver was one of the men who had been sitting in Junk Food. Repellent at first glance, but we had no choice. I told him the name of the street parallel to mine. I wanted to cover our tracks. My aunt and I started talking between ourselves in a whisper. I could feel her heart pounding. She could feel my heart pounding. Her hand was in mine. The driver drove at about ninety miles an hour on a road where soft rain was falling, some irritating music was playing on a half-broken radio-cassette, I felt the driver's eyes in his rear-view mirror, but I thought that in the circumstances that wasn't at all strange... My aunt was telling me something and I her, we told each other that everything was going to be OK, she told me how much she loved me, I told her how much I loved her, she told me everything was going to be OK, I told her that everything was going to be OK, I noticed that the driver was taking us the wrong way, rain was beating against the taxi window, but I thought the man was just adding kilometres so as to charge us more, maybe he wanted to enter that parallel road from the other direction to help us cover our tracks, the meter, I could see, was working according to a special tariff that Zagreb taxi drivers use when they want to rob someone, but I didn't say anything because I didn't care about the money at all. I didn't give a damn about money. We just had to get home and lock ourselves behind the burglar-proof door of my flat. The driver's mobile rang. My aunt and I held each other's hands. We kept chanting that everything was going to be just great.

'I'm bringing them both,' said the taxi driver. I thought I had heard wrong. My aunt made a face. What the fuck is the man saying, I wondered.

'They're both with me in the car.'

'Do you hear what I hear?' whispered my aunt.

'We're on our way,' said the driver. 'Why, I said I'd bring them both, here they are in the back.'

My aunt took her heavy fob of keys out of her handbag. I have no idea why she had those keys in her bag, they were the keys of her house and car in Australia... like a deus ex machina, a grasshopper had leapt into her hand. She opened the fob and placed it under the driver's chin.

'STOP!' she yelled at the same moment as I screamed 'STOP THE CAR!'

He stopped. We fell out. Ten minutes later, hiding in the doorway of an apartment block several hundred yards from the road, I called the police. We had to wait about forty minutes. They came, grinning, and asked us who had stolen our shoes and why we were all muddy. We told them what had happened. They didn't believe a single word.

That was definitely one of the toughest nights of my life. A simply terrible, appalling night. But even so, that night in Junk Food I had seen my tiger, furious and blazing with love.

Theological proof

Zoran Ferić

1 Lack of heart

Let's get this straight. In my lifetime I've tried lots of male sex organs: knotty, dumpy, crooked, bent downwards, bent upwards, straight as candles and soft as the soul, reddish, bluish and dark mauve, light as a chicken salami, darker, smaller, shaded with green, noble, flabby and abstract, moist, lank, flaky and shedding little bits of skin, fat and thin, little and large ... But none of them penetrated my heart.

When I grasped this, in my twenty-first year, I decided to exchange my lack of heart for a surplus of convertible currency and put out an ad offering my services as an escort lady. In the course of the last five years of my business I've tried a whole series of marketing strategies in advertising. I began philosophically: Let not *Kama Sutra* be a thing of the past, Lala Zuhra will revive it at last; went on psychotherapeutically: If pussy's on your mind by night and day, just give a call to Daisy May; and ended up poetically: Well-placed male, don't waste time, slender blonde female is waiting to chime.

When my best friend, who's engaged in the same business, asked me: 'What's this: "eats like a horse, barks like a dog and fucks like a rabbit"?' I knew at once: 'A member of parliament.'

'That makes our parliament a society for the protection of animals!' she explained.

That's because in our trade politicians are frequent customers, so we know all there is to know about them. Soldiers come as well, it's true. Soldiers, however, are incomparably more agreeable customers than members of parliament because they have smaller bellies. In truth, members of parliament have their good sides as well: they're old so they can't keep it up for long, and they don't usually smell. At least not of sweat and dirty socks, like labourers, Bosnians. They tend to smell of mothballs instead. My best friend says they also smell of wax, as though they were dead, but I think that's from the candles they light at Mirogoj cemetery, for their classmates.

I don't need to mention that in my five-year career I've tried just about everything, but the guy who called me that afternoon through the small ads was the strangest thing I had ever encountered. When I rang the bell, and the guy opened the door, I saw that he wasn't old, but he was fat. Something like forty-five, but weighing fifteen stone. In this line of work it's like that – if they're not old, they're fat. If their weight goes down, their years pile up and vice versa. A month ago I had a slender one, just eight stone, but he was eighty years old. We could have talked about his memories of Auschwitz.

2 Pyramids

When I entered the flat, the guy seemed familiar. As though I had seen him somewhere before. Only where? Otherwise, he looked respectable. Fat, yes, but quite well dressed: brown corduroy sports jacket, a black V-neck top underneath it, rimless glasses and a sparse little beard. He showed me into the living room and told me to sit down.

He brought a bottle of pinot noir from the kitchen and just one glass. I thought that was odd right away. Either he was a reformed boozer, I thought, or he's put something into it. When you do this work, however, you can't afford to be paranoid. So I let him pour me a glass and I sipped it. With pleasure, in defiance of everything. When he saw that I had settled in, he said:

'Wait here a moment, there's something I have to do!'

And he went into the other room. I noticed that he closed the door carefully.

OK. I turned on the television, sat down in the white leather armchair and sipped my pinot noir. I could have carried on like that until the day after tomorrow, but something was bugging me. What was the guy doing in the other room? What was it he had to do right now, when the time he was paying for was ticking by? And then it occurred to me that something wasn't quite right, that all was not as it should be. I can't say I didn't care, but I carried on sipping and watching television. It was a programme about models of pyramids. My old lady had a pyramid like that made of cardboard from the back of a calendar and she kept it under her bed to treat her rheumatism. On television they were saying that you could sharpen a razor by putting it inside a pyramid. And if you put a pyramid on your head, it acted on the brain and made you cleverer. That's why I'd spent the whole second semester of my first year of economics studying with the pyramid on my head, and the old lady went berserk because I had taken her pyramid, while Arap, a medical student who was servicing her at the time, wanted to use it to sharpen his razors.

When we met, the guy had told me that he worked as an administrator in a hospital for infectious diseases, but something didn't seem right to me. His mug was too familiar. And then I figured it out: infectious diseases, administrator, my foot! The man was a writer, he published newspaper columns. There was a photograph. And he had presumably lied to me because he was afraid I'd blackmail him as a public figure. Well, I was a public woman, and I didn't give a flying fuck what anyone thought of me. But OK, I told myself, it's 20 per cent more if you lie to me. And then I remembered that he hadn't even asked me about the price. This wasn't at all good.

3 The grey bundle

After a while, I don't know how much time had passed, I realised that I was looking at the pyramids, but I was really thinking about the guy in the other room. And my black forebodings returned. Matilda, who we called Sparrow, told us that she had just got undressed in the larder of some man who had ordered her through an advertisement, when she heard a noise. Not very loud, but powerful. Like a shot from a pistol with a silencer. She was petrified. First she called softly and then more loudly. But the guy didn't respond. Deathly silence. She put on her knickers and bra and began to look for him all through the flat. In the corridor was a shirt, but no sign of him, of course. In the bedroom trousers thrown over the bedside light; in the kitchen one sock; in the children's room another. Something really wasn't right. Finally she found him in the bathroom kneeling stark naked in front of the washing machine, counting the little holes in the drum. One, two, three... he'd completely lost the plot. He counted, but he couldn't work out where he had begun, all the little holes were the same, so he kept starting all over again. She got off lightly. The guy wasn't aggressive. But this one?

I was just thinking about that, about aggression, and when I raised my eyes from the screen, the guy was standing in front of me. I'd been miles away, I simply hadn't heard the door opening. I looked at him and I couldn't see how he had suddenly materialised. And then I noticed he was wearing those rubber gloves that are as stretchy as johnnies, and used by murderers in films. Terror. I think that something happened to my brain, a kind of paralysis, because I couldn't move. I saw and heard everything: the screen and the old woman shoving a sick mouse into a pyramid, the big ficus under the window, the little table with the wine and him, the guy in the gloves. Not a chance of moving, however, like in dreams.

Then the guy put a grey plastic bundle down on the table in front of me. It had a smiling woman with yellow hair and a check apron over her chest printed on it.

'Here are some rubber gloves for you,' he said. 'Be so kind as to put them on!'

He looked strange. The lines of his face seemed to be arguing with each other, and some furrows were deeper. Then he went back into the other room and closed the door behind him. I took off my shoes, put them in my handbag, turned up the volume on the television and made a dash for the door. I suddenly had a strong urge to get out. But the door was locked, and there was no sign of the key. It was getting dangerous.

4 Hiroshima

What started then, that sound, that was something unearthly. I think I'd heard it in a documentary about soldiers in a field hospital somewhere having their limbs cut off when they'd been damaged by shrapnel. I was sure it was an electric surgical saw. Because when doctors saw through something, first they slowly make a slit with a scalpel and then they cut deeper, and when they get to the bone they take that saw and in an instant slice through the bone. The sound caught me, barefoot, in the hall. I began to make my way slowly back to the living room. I didn't want the maniac to work out that I was petrified. Now I was convinced that he was going to chop me into pieces and jerk off into every separate part. I'd seen a cartoon like that in *Playboy*, the American edition, some twenty years before. Two guys with a bloody chain saw are standing over a woman they've just chopped up, blood up to their knees, idiotic faces, saliva dripping from their jowls, and one asks:

'Frank, do you think we should have raped her first?'

Fucking hell. At those moments I wanted to be like Stallone, Van Damme or the greatest hero of my youth, Bruce Lee, then I wouldn't be afraid of these pot-bellied cretins. I was afraid of maniacs when I was in elementary school too, but local ones, from the edge of town, the kind who flash at little girls in dark doorways. That's why my old lady signed me up for karate. There was that Japanese guy there, the trainer. I fell for him big time. How old would I have been? Twelve I suppose, I was in year six of elementary school. He was actually my first love. A guy thirty years old. Ever since then I've liked yellow skin best.

I remembered him when Matilda found me that other Japanese guy. The old one. He was some big fish in Deutsche Telekom. Japanese, working for Germans, pure bloody Nazism. Just then I was completely broke, however, so I said to Matilda: 'OK, I'll give him a blow job.' And Matilda told me that the guy was called Hushimato.

'As far as I'm concerned, he can be called Hiroshima. As long as he pays!'

We met at country restaurant, Hushimato the Japanese, nearly six feet tall. And he immediately kissed my hand. I don't know what had got into him, he was kissing my hand, and me a whore, in front of all those wankers in the restaurant. He must have thought I was a geisha. And so we sat down, ordered brandies, and Hushimato asked me in English whether I had any objection to him taking off my left shoe. I said I hadn't, and he ordered another brandy and tenderly took off my left shoe. And then he drank the brandy and asked me whether I had any objection to him taking off my right shoe. No, I said. He ordered another brandy and tenderly took off my right shoe. Then he asked me whether I had any objection to him placing my foot on that place. No, I said, and thought, This is going to be easy. And so he took hold of my left foot and began to rub it as though jerking off, and I immediately thought of those poor women of theirs whose feet are bound so that they fit into children's shoes. I saw that at the exhibition 'The Land of the Rising Sun', in the museum when we went with the school. I was afraid that he might bind my foot up, but he, the sick man, pushed his prick, through his trousers, into the gap between my first and big toes. I got it at once: a foot fetishist. That's probably a Japanese tradition. That's why they bind those poor women's feet.

He was doing that down there, while up here he smiled. The way the Japanese smile at everyone. I could feel that he was already hard and he had begun to water at the mouth. Then the main course arrived. The old man gobbled his food, while I jerked him off with my foot. I ran up and down his dick, and it was big. Not remotely Japanese. Then he ordered a fifth brandy and I realised that he was getting plastered and wanking in parallel. And so, with combined forces, we got him to come.

I felt moisture on my foot, through his trousers. How was he going to go to his business meeting, all smeared with sperm? And he wasn't completely sober any more either. At a certain point, however, he got up and went to the toilet. I waited. No sign. I waited some more, fifteen minutes passed, and there was no sign of him. It occurred to me that he had split, leaving me the bill for lunch. I wouldn't have been surprised. There are people like that. They fill their stomachs, climax, and leave. So I went down to the toilets and I saw the Japanese man. Fuck it, he was kneeling in front of the urinal. I thought he'd lost it, like that guy with the holes in the washing machine. I went closer and saw. He hadn't gone berserk: he'd thrown up in the urinal. And in doing so he had evidently thrown up his dentures as well. I was struck that he'd aimed at the urinal, pedantically, not beside it. It's not surprising they're the most successful nation. And there he was, in his elegant gear, one hand rooting around in the sick, looking for his teeth. Fuck it, not a single tooth of his own, just rubber and plastic. And his glasses had fallen off as well.

What could I do? With my stomach heaving, I rolled up the sleeve of my silk blouse, shoved my hand into the tepid vomit and felt around, looking for his teeth. And the vomit was like when I was a kid and shoved my hand into warm custard looking for little pieces of fruit, which my old lady used to spread over wafers for the cakes she made. I found his dentures and gave them a bit of a wash under the tap. But that wasn't the worst. The pig had shat himself too. He must have got the runs from the alcohol. It was dripping from him like chocolate milk, it was so thin... The stench was indescribable. My stomach rose to my throat. But what could I do? I cleaned him up above and below, put his teeth in and called an ambulance.

When the lads came with the ambulance, they put me and him into the car and drove us to the hospital. And then this other lad, a nurse, asked me what this old man, the Japanese, was to me. That made me wild. What business was it of his? The man had been taken ill, and every man's a man, even if he's Japanese. And then I said, I don't know what got into me:

'He's my father!... My old man! OK?'

He looked at me, then at the Japanese man, then at me, and he just didn't get it. I stroked the Japanese man's damp forehead, I felt sorry for him, and his eyes moistened because I had said he was my father. I realised: he understood our language, he'd understood everything, he just pretended he didn't. And I would have been quite overcome by tenderness for an older man, a stranger, and from another civilisation what's more, had I not noticed that other thing. I'm a professional, after all. At that word — father — he got hard again, all covered in vomit and shit as he was. And it stuck up under his wet trousers, like a bold samurai sword, that God had thrust into his bum when he was born.

5 The guided missile

Then the sound from the next room suddenly stopped. A ghastly silence. Then I realised that I was still sitting in a maniac's living room, with rubber gloves on my hands and my shoes in my handbag. I thought for a minute: he's tried out the saw, tested its speed, now he's turned it off so that I'm not scared when he summons me in to be cut up. That thought hadn't quite crossed my mind when I heard his voice from the other room:

'Would you come in now, miss?'

Fuck it, I was paralysed with fear. And then the door opened slowly. Like in horror films. I looked at the open door, but I couldn't stir, my legs had been severed. Then that fat guy in the bedroom, who I couldn't see, but I heard him, suddenly sneezed. And that freed me up a bit. That sneeze. It must have seemed human and real. I'd never heard maniacs sneeze in horror films. I got up and went towards the room. I wondered as I walked, should I say the Lord's Prayer, but I decided against it. First, it seemed a little inappropriate at this moment, and second, I'm not remotely religious. And when I entered the room, the scene was wild. I saw the fat man. He was quite naked down below, and on top he had a little white shirt, like a child's, which covered only the top of his chest and back, so that the folds of fat on his belly could be seen in profile. When he realised that I had come in, he stuck out his great behind, like the rear part of a half-pig, and shoved it in the air. First I saw that his skin round the hole was red. Then I noticed special shaving apparatus on the table. So that was the noise, not an electric saw. The guy had shaved his hole. This was fairly interesting. And then he said formally:

'Be so kind as to push your finger into my bum!'

That's just what he said: 'be so kind' and 'bum'. And I caught myself thinking that this wasn't quite the strangest thing I had done up to now, but it was pretty wild. I know people who even snort coke up their arseholes, they must prefer the bloodiness to nose snot. So I went over, stood behind him, and shoved my index finger inside. I thought about my late mother, who always told me not to point my finger at the neighbours because it was rude. When she came home from work, at the bank, she used to say: 'How was little pointy-finger today? Was he rude?' It would be hard for my old lady to imagine what I was doing with that index finger today. But as soon as I pushed it in, the guy squealed like a little pig and swore:

'Not dry, miss! Put some cream on first!'

It was only then that I noticed the Vaseline on the table. I rubbed it on to my finger, then began to push it slowly in. I had seen people in porn movies shoving their whole hands up women. And he said, as though my finger were a guided missile:

'Up a little, down a little, down, thaaat's it, now press a bit there!'

And I felt something thickened there, like a kind of knot, and thought: What's a writer doing with a knot in his bum? Maybe his balls are in the wrong place? And just then he said in a formal voice:

'Now press!'

And I pressed the fat man's thickening in his bum and hoped that he would come. But instead he picked up a little piece of glass from the table, like the ones we had at school for microscopes, and put it under his prick. Then he told me to press a bit harder. And I pressed harder, and he squealed and a few drops dripped on to the glass. I could see he hadn't come, it didn't look like sperm, and his prick was still standing up. However, he said:

'Thank you very much!'

He put the piece of glass carefully away in a little plastic box and began to get dressed, and instead of ass's ears, question marks stuck out of my head. What was all that about? If you ask me, it wasn't sex.

Of course, it wasn't sex for him either. The guy was obsessed with illnesses, or something like that, he kept going to doctors. He had a problem with his prostate, he said. Infections, thickening, that kind of thing. He kept having to go for check-ups and they kept taking samples. The nurse pressed something from behind, and something dripped out of his prick. And then they sent it away for analysis. Whenever they took a sample in the hospital, however, he got a hard-on. It was extremely awkward, of course. That was why he had stopped going to the hospital. He said he loved his wife, she was the only woman he screwed, and he paid whores only when he had to go for a prostate test and they needed a sample. Thank you, he said, all the best and every success in your work.

6 Faust

That afternoon I began to think about God. The real God, not the one who shoves samurai swords up Japanese bums. Before evening I had to do an old scholar who had once been a big fish in politics. Minister of higher education or something like that. I had inherited him from my best friend when she went to get married in Bjelovar to some old guy with a dive on the motorway to Osijek. The old man had asked me to come up to the Mirogoj cemetery, to the Ruđer Bošković Institute, because there was an office there. Apart from an office, the old phoney had Parkinson's and these were his very last shags. And towards the end of his life, something happened in his head and he turned to God. He said that science wasn't worth a piddling prick. I told him that about God. That God and I had never been on the same wavelength and that science was sufficient explanation of the world for me. Then he went quiet. Then in that silence he opened his fly and, with shaking hands, tucked his gristle away in my mouth.

So that autumn afternoon I thought about politics, science, God and my own position in the world. That is, a young girl reflects on her own failures most easily with an antique prick in her mouth.

Zoran Ferić

That's a very particular perspective.

Towards the end, when he was almost quite done, the old man said, as though some little lamps had been belatedly lit:

'Science is only the study of the mechanisms through which God governs the world.'

Fuck it, that hadn't occurred to me. And I said to myself: your life is proof of the existence of the Devil. So there must be a God somewhere as well. Just then the old man spilled himself into my throat.

Photo opportunity

Matt Thorne

Jeff got up from the table, went to the kitchen and scraped his fish and chips into the bin. Although he and Sophie taught at the same school, they were so busy during the day that the only time they got a chance to talk was when the pair of them sat down to eat in the evening. Every conversation seemed to end in an argument, agitating his sensitive stomach and making it impossible for him to finish his food. Tonight Jeff felt so angry and upset that he didn't even want to be in the same flat as Sophie any longer, and he went from the kitchen to the telephone, where he called his friend Arnold. Ten minutes later, they were in the pub.

'It's getting serious,' Jeff told Arnold. 'If we don't get away this summer that'll be it.'

Arnold nodded. He understood. He was in the same situation. The four friends rarely went on holiday. All teachers, they led a slightly more indulgent lifestyle than the rest of the school's staff, leaving them little money to go away. For three years they had suffered the embarrassment of having no traveller's tales for the start of term, and Arnold's wife Connie was as desperate as Sophie to get away.

Arnold sipped his lager and suggested, 'Why not take him up on his offer?'

This surprised Jeff. 'Do you want to?'

'I spoke to Greg. He couldn't believe you'd said no.'

Jeff and Arnold had the same Croatian student in their classes. On parents' evening, Zoran had marvelled at how much his son had learnt, and his deep affection for his teachers. Zoran told them he could arrange for them to spend a fortnight in Motovun, a medieval town in his homeland. Jeff had immediately refused, worried about accepting such a generous offer from a student's father. Arnold was better travelled than Jeff, but he didn't know anything about Croatia, and feared Motovun might not be such a great place to visit. The boy's father had been disappointed, but told them it would be no trouble if they changed their minds.

'OK,' said Jeff, 'speak to Zoran. See what you can fix up.'

When Jeff returned to his flat that night, he was expecting the argument to continue. The previous night he had come back from the pub after an evening with Arnold, and their argument had grown so heated that it ended with him smashing a table. But Sophie seemed calm, watching an episode of *Six Feet Under* on the small black television that stood on a wooden table at the end of their bed.

'I spoke to Arnold about Zoran's offer. We're going to reconsider.'

Sophie was so excited she flung herself up from the bed and into his arms, knocking him back on to their wooden floor. That night he had his first decent night's sleep in weeks, relaxed from the beer and pleased that his wife was no longer angry with him.

The trip took longer than they'd imagined. Zoran had sorted out all the accommodation, but had left the travel up to them. After scouring the Internet for the cheapest possible route, borrowing money from all four sets of parents, and staying in for a fortnight, they managed (with the helpful knowledge of Mr Gregg, the school's geography teacher) to get tickets to fly to Graz, travel through Austria and Slovenia to Zagreb, then take a coach to

Photo opportunity

Motovun. Jeff felt a strange sense of calm overtake him the moment they left England, and as they travelled through Austria he recalled an old fantasy of his to move to a small town where no one knew him or spoke his language and live an entirely isolated existence. He wondered whether his friends would understand why this seemed so appealing, but felt too nervous to share this with them. During the long train journey, every time they passed a border, the network provider changed on their mobile phones. Jeff was curious as to whether the Slovenian network would have a permanent record of the tiny amount of time his phone had been connected to their service.

When they arrived in Motovun, exhausted after a whole day, and much of the night, of travel, the friends discovered that Zoran had booked them into a hotel alongside a sulphur spring. Usually only the very old or the very sick came to his hotel, but once a year it was overrun by visitors to the Motovun film festival near by. When they checked in, Connie discovered that Zoran had arranged passes to the festival for them.

'Let's go,' cried an excited Sophie. She was the daughter of a lieutenant colonel and possessed seemingly inexhaustible energy.

'Fuck that,' said Arnold, 'I'm wasted.'

Sophie looked upset but didn't complain. Connie picked up her green-and-white laminated pass and examined it. In a conciliatory voice, she told Sophie, 'It's OK, it's on for several days.'

They went to their rooms and Jeff lay on the bed while Sophie unpacked. Before meeting Sophie, whenever he travelled, which was rarely, Jeff lived out of his suitcase. But Sophie had spent her adolescence shuttled between a succession of boarding schools and loved emptying suitcases into cupboards and wardrobes. Jeff was just thinking about going downstairs to the bar for a beer when there was a knock at the door.

'Arnold's had a wash and woken up a bit,' said Connie. 'Do you still want to go to that festival?'

To reach the film festival, the friends had to take a minibus from the hotel to the bottom of the mountain, and then switch to a larger coach for the rest of the journey. As they waited for the second ride, the clandestine air and excitable crowd, together with the fact that this was taking place in the middle of nowhere, reminded Jeff and Sophie of illicit parties they had gone to when they were younger, and they discussed their separate memories of such events.

Connie was a Spanish teacher, and like many bilingual people she could get by in several other languages. She told the others that there were many other nationalities, especially Italians, here. So far they had met no other English people, but when they reached the top of the mountain Sophie recognised, among the many people walking through the illuminated medieval settlement, a famous English film director. In England and America, this director – whose last film had been nominated for several Baftas and Oscars – would have been accompanied by a group of flunkeys and publicists, but here he was walking unrecognised among the crowd. What surprised them was that he was holding hands with a young Italian starlet. Sophie, the only member of the group totally au fait with the most recent film and gossip magazines, explained to the others that it had been rumoured that the actress and director were having an affair, although this story had been quashed when the director returned to his wife. Sophie told them that a photograph of the actress and director together would be worth several thousand pounds from a British tabloid newspaper. As she said this, Connie instinctively raised her camera and took the picture. Jeff expected the couple to immediately whip round, but they remained oblivious to the attention, no doubt assuming they were safe from paparazzi in this remote location.

The lower level was packed with thousands of people. They

Photo opportunity

passed a first row of cafés and shops where a group of people had
gathered to dance. Jeff strained to make out the lines, and heard
someone singing in English, but in a foreign accent, the lyrics *I have
no money/So visit me in your free time/I have no home/So visit me in
your dreams*. They continued through the crowds into the main
square. At the far end of the square was a DJ booth and one of the
many makeshift screens on to which films would be projected
throughout the weekend. They managed to buy beer – Arnold
remembered the word *pivo* from a school trip to Prague – but
when they tried to buy food they discovered that their money was
useless. The small yellow plastic trays of beef, chicken and chips
were being exchanged only for small white-and-green tickets.
Connie checked the bag she had been given with the laminated
passes at reception and discovered that she had several nights' worth
of tickets for each of them. They took their food and beer and went
to sit together at a small wooden table.

Jeff was staring at a small house with a brown roof. It was more
of a shack than a house, the roof tiles smoothed away into a dip by
centuries of rain, leaving it looking as if an elephant had sat on it.

'That house is amazing,' he said.

'Why?' asked Arnold.

'I don't know. But I want to buy it.'

Arnold laughed, and for the rest of the holiday they would all
refer to this shack as 'Jeff's house', taking several photographs of him
standing outside it. The area they were in was extremely busy, with
large groups of people eating, drinking and talking. Connie noticed
the director and the actress, sitting by a tree a couple of tables away
from them. 'Look,' she stage-whispered, 'they're back.'

For the rest of the evening the group talked of nothing else but
the photograph Connie had taken. They were so desperate for
money that even a thousand pounds split between them would've
made a big difference. Arnold kept insisting that if the couple had
come here together their affair was clearly no longer a secret and

the picture would be worthless. But the two women were convinced that the couple had come here without anyone knowing, probably as a farewell to their relationship. Jeff said if this were true they couldn't possibly expose them. It was immoral as well as unkind. Most of all, they worried about getting Zoran into trouble.

At twelve o'clock, Jeff and Arnold were feeling tired and wanted to catch the coach and minibus back to the hotel. Connie and Sophie were reluctant to leave, eager to watch a gypsy band that would be taking the stage at one o'clock. The excitable women had little sympathy for the men, but eventually (after a frustrated Arnold had started to walk off on his own) they agreed to return with them. The driver took for ever to get them home and they joked among themselves about his caution.

The following morning, Jeff felt Sophie get out of bed at an absurdly early hour. She left their hotel room and he tried to get back to sleep. When she returned, he barely followed what she was saying and had to force himself to concentrate on her words.

'I've got Connie's camera,' she told him. 'It's a digital picture so I can send it directly to the *Sun*, or the *Mirror*, if Connie and Arnold don't like the idea of selling something to the *Sun*, from the Internet exchange at the film festival. I'll call you later and let you know how much money I got.'

Jeff waved her away and went back to sleep. Two hours later, he was awoken again by a knock on the room door. He pulled on his boxer shorts and went to open it.

It was Connie. 'We asked this guy at breakfast and he said Rovinj's the best place for sunbathing and a swim. There's a bus there at ten o'clock.'

He scratched his head. 'Should we wait for Sophie to get back?'

'No, she said she'll come along later. She's not had much luck getting hold of anyone at the newspapers and she's waiting for someone to call her back.'

'OK.'

Jeff got dressed and the three of them went downstairs to wait for the bus.

Rovinj came as a surprise. They had been expecting a sandy beach, but instead they found something much more challenging. Instead of a beach there were small cliffs alongside the sea, with the occasional flat shelves where they could spread out. They found a space and unrolled their towels. Arnold raised his eyebrows at Jeff and nodded towards a couple sitting a short distance away. It was the director and the actress. Feeling guilty, Jeff said, 'Let's say hello.'

'No,' said Arnold, 'then they'll know it was us who sold the story.'

'Not necessarily,' Connie countered, 'just don't tell them we're at the film festival.'

The three friends approached the couple. Sophie had filled them in on both the director's and the actress's career the previous evening, so they were able to flatter them without seeming obsequious. At first, the couple seemed nervous, but slowly they began to grow increasingly friendly. The director was more wary than the actress, who seemed lonely and keen to talk. Despite their difference in social stature, they found they had a lot in common.

'My mother's a teacher,' the actress told them, pressing her toes against the rock. 'And it's something I've always considered as a possible alternative career. When all this comes to an end.'

'But that won't happen,' said Jeff, 'not now you're so well known.'

She smiled. 'Actresses like me don't get to work for long. Well, not unless we're prepared to appear in terrible erotic thrillers. I'm interested in making five great films and then retiring. I don't want to be an actress for ever.'

If Jeff had read this statement in print, he would've seen it as the insincere lie of someone who didn't want to be perceived as overambitious. But there was something about the actress, perhaps the fact that she was Italian, which made him believe she was telling the truth. Jeff was staring at the actress's toes when Arnold nudged him, pointing to a familiar figure on a nearby yacht, waving at them.

'Look,' said the director, 'it's Zoran.'

'Do you know him?' Jeff asked.

'Of course. He's a great mate of mine.'

Zoran soon came ashore and sat between the three teachers and the director and his girlfriend. 'So,' he asked, 'how do you like Croatia?'

'I love it,' said the director. 'You were totally right. It is one of the most beautiful places in the world.'

Zoran smiled. He was wearing brown sunglasses and his hair was wet. 'Yes.'

The director's voice became serious. 'Why didn't you tell me about your other friends?'

'Is it a problem?' Zoran asked.

The director looked awkward. 'You know how it is. If anyone in England found out about this weekend.'

Zoran put his arm around Jeff and Arnold's shoulders. 'You have nothing to worry about,' he told the director. 'These are people of the utmost moral fibre. You can trust them with anything. Isn't that right?' he asked Jeff.

Jeff nodded. His guilt was becoming unbearable. He looked at Arnold, who seemed similarly awkward. The two men exchanged a look, and realised they needed to get away to talk. Pretending they wanted a swim, they changed into their trunks and made their way down the rocks to the sea.

'What are we going to do?' Jeff asked.

'What can we do? We're fucked.'

Before they could talk further, they noticed Zoran and the actress making their way towards them. The actress was wearing an elegant fifties-style white swimsuit. 'Christ,' said Arnold, 'that's a picture I'd pay for.'

'Make the most of it,' said Jeff, 'I doubt this will be a lasting friendship.'

On the train to Zagreb, Sophie had pulled Jeff's swimming trunks from his suitcase and displayed them to Connie and Arnold, prompting considerable amusement. Fire-engine red, they were far more revealing than Arnold's baggy, plaid swimming shorts. Yesterday he had shrugged off their jokes, unconcerned about looking stupid in front of his friends. But now that this glamorous actress was coming into the water with him, he wished he had chosen more carefully.

Zoran and the actress reached the two men. Jeff flinched as the actress took his hand. 'Can't I jump in with you?' she asked, sounding hurt.

'Of course,' he said, and they did so together. The water felt wonderful. As they swam out into the sea, the actress touched him again.

'Let's float on our backs and talk for a while.'

'OK,' he replied.

'I'm sorry if we seem stand-offish,' she said. 'It's just a surprise…'

'You're not stand-offish,' said Jeff, 'you've been very friendly.'

She ignored this. 'We've been through a lot lately. His wife tried to commit suicide just before we came here. If she knew he was here with me…'

Jeff couldn't answer, wondering if it was possible to feel any more ashamed than he did now.

'Pppft,' she spluttered, as the water entered her mouth, 'you don't want to know my problems. Us actresses, we thrive on drama. It must seem such a cliché to you.'

Jeff didn't answer. The two of them rolled on to their fronts and swam for a while, then returned to the rocks and climbed from the water.

Matt Thorne

'You seem so confident,' she said, with awe in her voice. 'I wish my life was like yours. Are you married?'

He nodded.

'Where's your wife? Didn't she want to come away with you?'

'No, no,' he said, 'she's here.'

'In Croatia?'

'Yes. But she wanted to stay in Motovun today.'

'Ah, yes,' said the actress, 'there are some good films on today.'

Zoran and Arnold emerged from the water and started walking up the rocks behind them. Connie remained with their belongings, deep in conversation with the dark-haired director. They spread out their towels and sat down. Moments later, Jeff's mobile rang.

It was Sophie. She sounded emotional. Jeff prepared himself for hearing about the betrayal. 'I couldn't do it,' she told him, 'I'm sorry, I just couldn't. I know we're desperately in need of the money – this last year has been such a grind – but it felt so wrong. They're people too, and entitled to their privacy. Do you think Arnold and Connie will be angry with me?'

'Relax.' He smiled, looking round at his friends' anxious faces. 'I don't think they'll be angry at all.'

Afterword

by the Editors

This anthology is the result of a lasting relationship between a diverse group of Croatian authors and the British writers they have invited to visit their country in recent years. Borivoj Radaković has, for many years, translated English-language fiction into Croatian and has been instrumental in creating an appetite for a certain strand of British fiction in Croatia. The Croatian writers were part of a group called FAK, the Festival of Alternative Literature (Književnost). They had questioned the literatures that dominated Croatian culture during the late 1980s and 1990s. They had rejected both post-modern irony and nationalism – a process that was encouraged by exposure to international literature and especially to trends emerging in British fiction such as the short story project *All Hail the New Puritans*.

Over several years, all the British authors in this collection were invited to Croatia, where they were welcomed by the FAK group, and where they took part in events and festivals in front of huge audiences all over the country, as well as in Novi Sad and Belgrade in Serbia. After these visits, the editors of this anthology (along with some of the authors, particularly Ben Richards) decided to cement this bond, to take a 'snapshot' of the networks that continue to evolve between Britain and Croatia, and to present new works of fiction to the reading publics of both countries with this collection. The visits took place mainly between 2000 and 2003, and the stories were written in 2003–2004. This anthology is being published simultaneously in Britain and Croatia.

About the contributors

Vladimir Arsenijević was born in 1965 in Pula, Croatia. He lives in Belgrade and works as an editor in the publishing house Rende. His published works, which deal with the political and social environment, include the novels *U potpalublju (In the Hold)*, a fierce critique of Slobodan Milošević's regime and winner of the prestigious NIN prize, *Anđela (Angela)*, *Cloaca Maxima* and *Ismail*, and *Mexico*, a war diary.

Nicholas Blincoe was born in 1965 in Rochdale, England. He lives in London where he works as a novelist and critic. His published titles include *Acid Casuals, Jello Salad, Manchester Slingback, The Dope Priest, White Mice* and *Burning Paris*. He co-edited the short story collection *All Hail the New Puritans*.

Jelena Čarija was born in 1980 in Trogir, Croatia, and currently studies production at the Drama and Film Academy in Zagreb. Her challenging novel *Klonirana (Cloned)* has made her one of Croatian literature's best new young voices.

Anna Davis was born in 1971 in Kent. She now lives in London and works part-time for Curtis Brown Literary Agency. Her novels include *The Dinner, Melting* and *Cheet*.

Zoran Ferić was born in 1961 in Zagreb. He currently works as a teacher of Croatian at a secondary school and writes a column for the weekly magazine *Nacional*. His published work includes the

About the contributors

acclaimed short story collection *Mišolovka za Walta Disneya (A Mousetrap for Walt Disney)*. Winner of a number of literary awards, he is one of the most widely read of Croatian writers. His work includes *Anđeo u offsajdu (An Angel in Offside)*, a novel, *Smrt djevojčice sa žigicama (Death of the Girl with Matches)*, and a collection of his columns *Otpusno pismo*.

Salena 'Saliva' Godden was born in 1972 in Margate. She lives in London. A poet, writer, performer and broadcaster, she presents shows on radio and television. Her stories and poetry have been published in numerous collections including *Tell Tales, Velocity, Vox'n'Roll, IC3: The Penguin Book of New Black Writing, Oral, Girlboy* and *The Fire People*.

Niall Griffiths was born in 1966 in Liverpool and has lived on a mountain in mid-Wales for thirteen years. His published works include the novels *Grits, Sheepshagger, Kelly & Victor, Stump* and *Wreckage*. He has also written a number of radio plays and regularly reviews books and restaurants. *Further Education*, a collection of short stories, and *Runt*, a novella, will be published in the near future.

Miljenko Jergović was born in 1966 in Sarajevo. A versatile and provocative writer and journalist, he has won many prizes in Croatia and internationally. Best known for his short stories and novels, his work includes three story collections, *Sarajevski Marlboro (Sarajevo Marlboro), Mama Leone* and *Historijska Čitanka (History Textbook)*, and the novels *Dvori od oraha* and *Inšallah Madona, Inšallah*, as well as poetry, a play and a novella. He currently works as a journalist for the weekly magazine *Globus*.

Toby Litt was born 1968 in Bedford and lives in London. His published work includes the short story collections *Adventures in Capitalism* and *Exhibitionism*, and the novels *Beatniks, Corpsing,* and *deadkidsongs*, translated as *Pjesme Mrtvih Klinaca, Finding Myself* and *Ghost Story*.

Gordan Nuhanović was born in 1968 in Vinkovci, Croatia. He graduated in journalism and works as a freelance journalist. His published works include the short story collections *Liga za opstanak (League for Survival)* and *Bitka za svakog čovjeka (Struggle for Each Man)*.

Edo Popović was born in 1957 in Livno, Bosnia and Hercegovina. He was one of the writers who influenced the generation of the late 1980s, chiefly with his collection *Ponoćni boogie (Midnight Boogie)*. Other works include *San žutih zmija (Dream of Yellow Snakes)* and *Koncert za tequilu i aspirin (Concert for a Tequila and Aspirin)*, and *Kameni pas (Stone Dog)*.

Borivoj Radaković was born in 1951 in Zemun, Serbia and Montenegro. Working as a writer, translator and journalist in Zagreb, he was one of the founders of FAK, the influential literary festival in Croatia in 2000. His linguistically experimental work includes the novel *Sjaj epohe (The Brilliance of the Epoch)*, and short story collections *Ne, to nisam ja – da, to nisam ja (No, this is not me – yes, this is not me)* and *Porno*, five plays and non-fiction, *Visitor's Book*, published in English in 2003, as well as *Sredina naprijed! (Pass Down Inside the Carriage!)*, a collection of essays and travelogues.

Zorica Radaković was born in 1963 in Sinj, Croatia. A full-time writer, she has published poetry, prose and plays, including *Svaki dan je sutra (Each Day is Tomorrow)*, her first work that appeared in 1983. Her play *Susjeda (Neighbour)* was internationally acclaimed and her radio plays are frequently performed on Croatian Radio – Zagreb.

Ben Richards was born in Burnley, Lancashire, in 1964. He lives and

About the contributors

works in London. His published works include *Throwing the House out of the Window, Don't Step on the Lines, The Silver River, A Sweetheart Deal* and *The Mermaid and the Drunks*. Ben Richards is also a screenwriter for the hit BBC TV show *Spooks* and Channel 4 television's *No Angels*.

Matt Thorne was born in 1974 in Bristol. He lives in London and writes full-time. Among his published works are the novels *Tourist, Eight Minutes Idle, Dreaming of Strangers, Pictures of You, Child Star* and *Cherry*. He co-edited the short story collection *All Hail the New Puritans*.

Goran Tribuson was born in 1948 in Bjelovar, Croatia, and teaches at the Drama and Film Academy in Zagreb. Author of more than a dozen screenplays and thirty works of fiction, including *Snijeg u Heidelbergu (Snow in Heidelberg)* and *Povijesti pornografije (History of Pornography)*, he ranges from crime fiction to humorous accounts of a rock-and-roll youth. He has won all of Croatia's major literary prizes.

Tony White was born in 1964 in Farnham, Surrey. He currently lives and writes in London, where he also works for Arts Council England and is literary editor of the *Idler* magazine. His published works include *Foxy-T* and *Charlieunclenorfolktango*. He edited the short story collection *Britpulp!* and has been editor and publisher of the samizdat imprint, Piece of Paper Press, since 1994.

John Williams was born in 1961 in Cardiff, Wales, where he now lives and works. His published works include the non-fiction titles *Into the Badlands, Bloody Valentine* and the novels *Faithless, Five Pubs, Two Bars and A Nightclub, Cardiff Dead, The Prince of Wales* and *Temperance Town*. He edited the short story collection *Wales, Half Welsh*.

Mercedes-Benz
Letters to Hrabel

Paweł Huelle

In the Polish city of Gdansk, our narrator Paweł tells of the driving lessons he took in the early 1990s, shortly after the end of communism. As he struggled with the tiny Fiat's gearbox, causing chaos while stalled at a crossroads, Pawel entertained his instructor Miss Ciwle with stories of his grandparents before the war and of his father in the 1970s, centred on their ownership of Mercedes-Benz cars – the outings, the races, the crashes and the inevitable repairs.

Based on fact and illustrated with personal photographs, these tales contrast the golden era of Poland's pre-war independence with the dismal communist years, and with the uncertain new chapter in the country's history that had only just begun when Paweł tells of learning to drive. With elegant brilliance, Huelle creates a touching portrait of three generations amid life-changing historical events.

White Raven

Andrzej Stasiuk

In the late 1980s a group of young men in their thirties leave Warsaw for a few days in the mountains, partly out of boredom, partly for an adventure. Their plans go badly wrong: they get lost, argue, and finally accidentally kill a border guard. Flight is now their only option... extreme flight through a totally inhospitable snowscape.

External landscapes and internal mindscapes blend as each man confronts his own life and most secret fears. *White Raven* explores the universal themes of lost youth and friendship against the backdrop of a rapidly changing society. The novel presents an array of finely crafted characters and a rare, if not first, sympathetic portrayal of a gay man in contemporary Polish literature.

'Like *The Big Chill* rewritten by Camus and Kundera'
Independent on Sunday

'A claustrophobic space seamed with an unrelenting menace'
The Times

'Amongst the most beautiful and influential prose works written after the political change of 1989 when Poland finally regained its freedom' *Independent*

Winner of the Nobel Prize for Literature

'**Elfriede Jelinek** is awarded the Nobel Prize for Literature for her musical flow of voices and counter-voices in novels and plays that with extraordinary linguistic zeal reveal the absurdity of society's clichés and their subjugating power' *The Nobel Prize Academy*

The Piano Teacher

'As a portrait of repressed female sexuality and a damaged psyche, *The Piano Teacher* glitters dangerously' *Observer*

'Her work tends to see power and aggression as the driving forces of relationships, in which men and parents subjugate women. But as an admirer of Bertold Brecht, she sometimes brings to her dramas a touch of vaudeville' *Guardian*

'With formidable power, intelligence and skill she draws on the full arsenal of derision. Her dense writing is obsessive almost to the point of being unbearable. It hits you in the guts, yet is clinically precise' *Le Monde*

'Jelinek's fragmented style blurs reality and imagination, creating a harsh, expressionistic picture of sexuality' *Scotland on Sunday*

Lust

'A thorough rubbishing of romantic love, *Lust* is intricately written with a tumbling pace, sustained and effective word-play and plenty of sharp, cynical authorial observation. More than good' *List*

Wonderful, Wonderful Times

'The writing is so strong, it reads as if it wasn't written down at all, but as if the author's demon spirit is entering first a boy and then a girl, a structure, a thing, a totality, to let it speak its horrible truth' *Scotsman*

Women as Lovers

'A chilling and truthful vision of women's precarious position in a society still dominated by money and men' *Kirkus Reviews*